LADY GOLD INVESTIGATES ~ VOLUME 5

A SHORT READ COZY HISTORICAL 1920S MYSTERY
COLLECTION

LEE STRAUSS

NORM STRAUSS

la
plume
PRESS

Library and Archives Canada Cataloguing in Publication

Title: Lady Gold investigates : a short read cozy historical 1920s mystery collection / Lee Strauss.

Names: Strauss, Lee (Novelist), author.

Description: Short stories. | Complete content: v. 5. The case of the murderous wife -The case of the blind reporter.

Identifiers: Canadiana (print) 20190131608 | Canadiana (ebook) 20190131624 | ISBN 9781774092552 (v. 5 : hardcover) | ISBN 9781774092545 (v. 5 : softcover) | ISBN 9781774092576 (v. 5 : IngramSpark softcover) | ISBN 9781774092538 (v. 5 : Kindle) | ISBN 9781774092569 (v. 5 : EPUB) Classification: LCC PS8637.T739 L34 2019 | DDC C813/.6—dc23

SUMMARY

Lady Gold Takes The Case in this 5th volume of Ginger Gold's popular short story mystery series! Join Mrs. Ginger Reed~aka Lady Gold, as she adventures with her new employee, Magna Jones, a tough-as-nails colleague Ginger worked with during the Great War, to unravel these enigmatic mysteries.

Lady Gold Investigates Volume Five presents *The Case of the Blind Reporter* and *The Case of the Murderous Wife*.

*This short story set jumps ahead to 1927 after book 20, *Murder at the Boxing Club*.

~~~

———

This book has been edited and proofed, but typos are like little gremlins that like to sneak in when we're not looking. If you spot a typo, please report it to: **admin@leestraussbooks.com**

THE CASE OF THE BLIND REPORTER

*W*ith her little Boston terrier, Boss, trotting happily along by her feet on his leash, Mrs. Ginger Reed stepped out of her Regent Street dress shop, Feathers & Flair, and made her way around the corner to her office of Lady Gold Investigations on Watson Street. It was a short jaunt, but time enough to get her mind off the everyday activity of running a clothing boutique and onto the business of solving mysteries. Though passionate about both, it did require a certain "shifting of gears" (to use a mechanic's term, and Ginger was fond of mechanical science) to move between the two.

"Hurry along, Bossy. Magna is going to be arriving soon, and it's almost time for a cup of tea. I can't let her beat me to the kettle."

The city streets were busy with horse-drawn carriages, motor cars, and lorries jostling about for a right of way. The pavement was congested with pedestrians—businessmen wearing trench coats and trilby or bowler hats, and fashionably dressed ladies showing off their fur-trimmed winter coats—Ginger had some difficulty keeping Boss from getting underfoot. Her office entrance was in sight and soon she'd be able to take refuge in the peace and quiet not found at her dress shop or her residence at Hartigan House.

She approached the set of stairs that led to the lower-level office—formerly a shoe repair shop, but one would never know the history of the space now that Ginger had had it completely repainted and redecorated—and paused as a taxicab came to a stop directly in front of the building. A man slowly climbed out of the back seat. He wore sunglasses, an accessory Ginger adored but which had yet to become common in ordinary society. They often signalled a status of wealth or being a celebrity, and had come into vogue with American film stars who now dominated magazine covers and train station billboard adverts.

Ginger didn't recognize the face of this man.

Tall and slender, he looked to be in his mid-forties and wore an expensive-looking overcoat and a trilby hat. He stood oddly motionless for a moment, staring straight ahead and tapping his walking cane idly on the paving stones. The taxicab driver walked quickly around the back of the vehicle and gently grabbed the stranger by the elbow.

He was blind.

Together, the blind man and the cabbie slowly started walking towards Ginger who politely stepped aside in anticipation of their passing. She took the three steps down to the door and inserted her key, only to find the door already unlocked.

Magna had beaten her to it again.

Just as she was about to turn the doorknob she heard the cabby say, "Right 'ere, Mr. Farnsworth. *Lady Gold Investigations.* It says so right 'ere on the door."

Ginger turned to the voice and said, "I'm Lady Gold. Can I be of assistance?"

"This is jolly good timing," the blind man returned. "Yes, I would like a word with you please, if you have the time."

"Of course," Ginger said. "Please mind the steps. There are three."

The man took the rail with one hand, then shook his shoulder to release the cabby's hold on his elbow. "I can take it from here, my man." He reached into his pocket and produced payment held out on his palm, which the cabby was quick to take.

"You are inside a small foyer," Ginger said. "There are two steps to the inside door. Can I assist you?"

The man smiled. "I never refuse an offer of aid from a lady with a voice as lovely as yours."

Ginger ignored the inappropriate response and took the man's elbow. The bell above the door chimed softly. With his cane tapping from side to side as he walked, Ginger led the man through the double glass doors that opened into the office area.

"Two more steps and you will encounter a chair," Ginger said. Magna Jones stared at her with her steely-blue eyes, one dark brow arched high. Ginger shrugged one shoulder, then, as the man settled into a wine-coloured leather-backed chair, said, "As you know, I'm Lady Gold, also known as Mrs. Reed. Present is my assistant Miss Jones. And you are Mr. Farnsworth? I overheard your driver mention your name."

"Yes," the man cleared his throat, "Mr. Roland Farnsworth." He held out a hand. "Pleased to meet you."

Ginger accepted the handshake with her gloved hand. "Likewise."

Magna cleared her throat. "I wasn't aware we had an appointment this morning."

"We didn't, before, but Mr. Farnsworth has just arrived to see us, so now we do," Ginger said as she hung her coat on the rack, removed her gloves and hat, and sat down behind her walnut desk. She relieved Boss of his leash, and he nosed his dog bed, then curled up in it.

"So, now then, Mr. Farnsworth," Ginger started, "what can we do for you today?"

He raised his chin. "Have you heard of me?"

"Should we have?" Ginger asked politely.

"I would imagine that someone in your line of work would keep up with the news."

Magna sniffed, her feathers ruffled. "Are you a journalist? I'm afraid, I don't recall your byline."

The man shook his head weakly. "It's of no consequence, at least not anymore." Raising a shaky hand he took hold of the round frames of his sunglasses, removing them from his face.

Ginger held in a gasp as she shared a sharp look with her assistant. She and Magna had seen a lot of terrible injuries during the war years when both of them were active members of the secret service, but

Ginger couldn't recall seeing anything like this before. Mr. Farnsworth's eyes were without irises or pupils, completely white except for webs of red veins that spread across them.

"I want . . ." Mr. Farnsworth's voice cracked. "I want you to help me find the person who did this."

Magna scowled. "Someone *did* that to you?"

Mr. Farnsworth nodded. "A devious attack."

Ginger stared at the man's eyes and the scarring in the soft tissue underneath them. "How long have you been blind?"

"I suffered partial blindness in 1917 at the Somme." Mr. Farnsworth returned his sunglasses to his face. "I served in the infantry until our unit was heavily bombed. A short section of rough timber used to reinforce our trench struck me on the back of the head."

"A sharp blow can damage fragile nerves and blood vessels in the brain that are used for visual processing," Magna said.

Ginger nodded at the assessment. She'd heard of the phenomenon.

"That's correct, Miss Jones," Mr. Farnsworth said. "I could still make out shapes and shadows, but not much else. I couldn't read. I had to walk with one of these blasted canes . . ." He tapped his cane on the floor with agitation. "I could get around on my own if I walked very slowly, but even the thickest spectacles didn't help."

"I'm so sorry," Ginger said, then asked, "Would you care for a cup of tea?"

Mr. Farnsworth nodded. "That would be splendid, thank you."

Magna left for the kitchenette, situated on the other side of a thin wall, perfect for listening in on conversations as they continued in the office area.

A moment of quiet passed before Mr. Farnsworth started again. "After the war, the future looked bleak for a man like me, but then a friend gave me a new type of typewriter. That gift saved my life, I think."

"A typewriter for a blind man?" Ginger asked.

"Yes. Each key was embossed with raised dots."

Ginger understood. "Braille, yes."

"I received instruction in Braille after the war, so I could already read it. It didn't take long to learn to type as well. You see, I always had an interest in journalism and . . ."

"That's where I know you from!" Ginger snapped her fingers. "Of course, Roland Farnsworth from *The News Standard Weekly*."

The man scoffed as if to say, *finally*. "Guilty as charged."

Magna returned with a tea tray and looked questioningly at Ginger.

"We have a bit of a celebrity in our office, Magna," Ginger explained. "This man is well known for his exclusive interviews with celebrity figures who don't usually give a lot of time to the press. Interviews that many journalists would envy."

"Is that so?" Magna said, her voice flat. She set the tea tray on Ginger's desk, and Ginger took on the task of pouring. "Do you take sugar, Mr. Farnsworth? I'm afraid we only have condensed milk in this office."

"Condensed milk is fine, Mrs. Reed," he responded. "Thank you."

Once everyone had settled with their tea and taken their first sip, Ginger said, "I've read many of your pieces, Mr. Farnsworth. You have quite a catalogue of impressive interviews."

Magna jumped in without letting the journalist relish the praise. "Really? With whom?"

"Oh, Charlie Chaplin for one," Ginger said. "George Gershwin, Pablo Picasso, and that American architect . . ." She inclined her head and asked, "What was his name?"

THE CASE OF THE BLIND REPORTER

"Frank Lloyd Wright," Roland Farnsworth answered. "But one of the hardest was my interview with Percy Fawcett, the famous British explorer who disappeared a couple of years ago. I had to travel all the way to Brazil to get that one. The Shah of Iran was also not an easy one to get either. He finally agreed, but I had to shower him with gifts first."

"Not bad for a man who can barely see," Magna said wryly.

"For this job, Miss Jones, the ability to ask good questions is more important than my sight," Mr. Farnsworth said. "You aren't alone in your scepticism. My detractors would say it was because of my handicap that I was granted these interviews, a mix of pity and bemusement on the part of the interviewee. I suppose they might be correct in that regard, but I prefer to think of it as my even-handedness and my insightful style of interviews. I always get interesting information without being unnecessarily invasive."

"Is there a Mrs. Farnsworth?" Magna asked. Her grin was sly, and Ginger pondered the irony that her assistant's steely gaze, known to unnerve the most steadfast character, had no power in this instance. Magna continued, "Behind many a successful man there is a woman to inspire and challenge."

Roland Farnsworth's eyebrows jumped in surprise. He shifted uncomfortably in his chair and cleared his throat.

"No, I've never married. So, as strange as it might seem, I have managed to struggle on without the benefit of a woman's *inspiration*."

Ginger was used to reading peoples' intentions and emotions by noting certain eye movements: the sudden enlarging of the pupil, a twitch, a rapid blinking . . . a type of physical language that people spoke without intending to, and it often gave away what they were secretly feeling. It was a bit disconcerting in this case to be staring at her own reflection in a pair of darkened spectacles.

Magna pressed on. "You've never had a special lady in your life?"

Ginger grimaced at the brashness of Magna's technique, but her assistant wasn't wrong to enquire. Spouses or spurned lovers were known to do terrible things.

Mr. Farnsworth exhaled, his lips moving as he deliberated. "There was one. I might as well tell you about her since I imagine you'll learn about her anyway. Sophie Radford. Our dalliance was short-lived." His lip pulled up on one side. "It didn't help that she was already married."

A round of sipping and clinking of teacups against their corresponding saucers took place before Mr. Farnsworth continued, "I looked into you, Mrs. Reed. We journalists are good at that sort of thing. I know that you had the title of Lady Gold because you were married to Daniel, Lord Gold, but he, sadly, passed away in the Great War. You are now married to a Chief Inspector from Scotland Yard."

"Yes, that's right," Ginger said, unsure if she should be impressed or annoyed. What other facts and foibles had he learned about her?

"That's one of the reasons I've come to you, Mrs. Reed," Mr. Farnsworth added. "Your affiliation with the police could be helpful. You see, I personally don't trust them for reasons I prefer not to explain, but I do realize they have resources that might be useful."

"Before I can be of any help," Ginger said, "and I haven't agreed to anything yet, I would like to hear the story of what happened to your eyes, to bring them to this state of damage."

Mr. Farnsworth adjusted his sunglasses. "Three weeks ago, I was attacked."

"Acid," Magna said.

With a nod, Mr. Farnsworth confirmed Magna's presumption. "The doctors believe it was an ammonia solution." He turned his head towards her but appeared to be talking to a spot on the wall beside her head. "Like the kind you would find in certain cleaning products. Easy enough to get."

"How did it happen?" Ginger asked. "Did someone splash it in your face?"

"No. This was planned aggression. I was rendered unconscious, probably with chloroform or something similar. The poison was sprayed into my eyes. It happened in my flat in the middle of the night while I was sleeping."

Magna slapped her thigh, which was protected only by the wool fabric of her tweed skirt. "*Mon dieu!*"

Ginger furrowed her brows.

"This to me seems like a criminal case, Mr. Farnsworth, clear and simple. Someone assaulted you, causing grievous bodily harm. Is the investigation still open?"

"No. There is no investigation. I haven't gone to the police."

"Why ever not?" Ginger said, surprised. "The police should be involved."

Mr. Farnsworth leaned forward in his chair, his hand propped on the top of his cane. "My mother was robbed last year. All the family jewels were stolen including some very precious items given to her by my late father. The only suspect the police could come up with after two months of investigation was my brother, even though Clive had no motive whatsoever. They actually put out a warrant for his arrest until they finally realized he was in Manchester on a business trip for an entire week around the date the jewels were stolen. The police are inept, Mrs. Reed, perhaps with your own husband as the exception."

Ginger could hardly come to the police's defence as many cases remained unsolved and corruption wasn't unheard of, but like Basil, there were many on the force who had taken the job for the right reasons. However, the grimace on Mr. Farnsworth's face told her that he wasn't ready to listen to a defence.

"My neighbour and the hospital staff are really the only ones who know what happened," Mr. Farnsworth said. "These sunglasses are a good way to hide my disfigurement from shop assistants and taxicab drivers, and even my own colleagues, though . . ."

"Though?" Ginger prompted.

"Though . . ." Mr. Farnsworth once again slowly removed his sunglasses and faced Ginger directly. "I suspect there is one among them who isn't fooled by these glasses."

Ginger glanced at Magna who gave a subtle nod.

"Mr. Farnsworth," Ginger said, "I will need a list of names."

2

The next morning, Ginger set out in her 1924 pearly-white Crossley sports tourer. She left Boss in the care of the staff at Hartigan House. As her pet was getting older it was becoming more and more apparent that he didn't tolerate cold weather as well as he used to, and today was very brisk. Felicia, Ginger's sister-in-law from her first marriage, had knitted Bossy a very nice woollen sweater, but unfortunately the dog didn't like wearing it and had somehow got hold of it with his teeth and unravelled the thing.

Ginger wore a red-and-black wool day frock today along with a pair of fur-lined gloves to keep out the chill from the wind. The car's convertible top was up, but the wind still pushed in through the window frames as she drove to the offices of *The News Standard Weekly*. Since the police had never been involved, she would have to start from scratch and hope a lead would present itself. The list of possible suspects that Roland Farnsworth had given them was rather short. The man claimed he had very few enemies, which in Ginger's mind was unusual for anyone in the public eye, much less a journalist. He was either a veritable paragon of virtue and affability or he wasn't aware of how he was perceived by others. At any rate, Ginger would do her best to get to the bottom of things.

Magna was on a mission, as well. With Roland Farnsworth's approval, she was going to search his flat. Magna happened to be an excellent investigator when it came to searching for clues at the scene of a crime. This was owing, in part, to her time spent as an agent for the Belgian spy network during the war, and in part to her natural curiosity. Something was always left behind. It was a matter of knowing where to look.

However, the more time passed, the more likely it was for evidence to disappear. There was no doubt that this case would be challenging.

The offices of *The News Standard Weekly* were located on Fleet Street just a few doors down from the Law Courts branch of the Bank of England. Parking the Crossley nearby—that tree she just missed seemed to come out of nowhere!—Ginger entered the building and quickly found the right floor. As soon as she stepped out of the lift, she could hear the clicking of typewriter keys and the inevitable ringing of the bell when the carriage had reached the end. The wood-panelled room had rows of desks tucked together side by side, each with a man slouched over as he worked.

At a reception desk at the entrance sat an attractive, blond woman who responded to Ginger's request to see Mr. Richard Pottinger, one of the top correspondents, with a breathy, "I'll let him know you're here."

A short time later, Ginger was shown to a room adjoining the journalists' room and asked to wait. She took a seat on one of the wooden ladder-back chairs and took out her notepad. Soon, a slim man in his mid-forties appeared. He wore wire-framed spectacles and was dressed in a white shirt with a polka dot bow tie, and black braces holding up grey woollen trousers.

"Hello. I'm Richard Pottinger." Curiosity crossed his face as he shook Ginger's hand. "You wanted to see me."

"Thank you for your time, Mr. Pottinger. I'm Mrs. Reed, though I'm also known as Lady Gold from Lady Gold Investigations."

"Yes, of course. Lady Gold. I've heard of you. I'm pleased to finally make your acquaintance." He took a seat opposite Ginger. "I see you have your notepad out. I'm usually the man doing that." He chuckled. "It looks like I'm the one being interviewed this time, though I can't imagine why."

"I'm investigating a recent incident involving a work colleague of yours, a Mr. Roland Farnsworth."

"Farnsworth?"

"The one and the same. Mr. Farnsworth hired me to look into a recent unfortunate event."

"Is that so?"

"Indeed. Can I count on your discretion, out of professional courtesy?"

Mr. Pottinger scratched his nose. "Well, now you've certainly piqued my curiosity, Mrs. Reed. How about we make a deal. I'll help you with your case and you give me an exclusive when the story— and it sounds like a story—breaks."

"Very well," Ginger said, "though I can't always control how information makes its way into the public. But you can count on me to come to you first with whatever I find. Do you have your diary handy?"

After a pause, Mr. Pottinger darted out of the room. Ginger could see him jog to his desk in the journalist's office, retrieve a leather-bound book from the drawer, then jog back. "What am I looking for?"

"The fifteenth of February."

Mr. Pottinger thumbed through the pages. "That was a Wednesday. I often go out to the cinema. The Phoenix in East Finchley usually."

"Were you there that night?"

"According to this, I was."

"What was showing?"

"*The King's Highway*, I think. Yes it was *The King's Highway*. That was a great film."

"Were you alone?"

"You know, Mrs. Reed, I am going to stop right here until you tell me what this is about. I feel like I'm being interrogated, and you're not a police constable."

"That's fair enough. Mr. Farnsworth was attacked on that night. I'm simply ruling you out, before I decide if I can trust you."

Mr. Pottinger's brows arched on his high forehead. "Attacked? That's why the bloke's been absent. Not to be insensitive, but Farnsworth has a way of taking over a room. It's been rather, shall I say, *calm*, these last few weeks."

Ginger was very much interested in learning about Mr. Farnsworth's character from the perspective of his colleagues, but she would save those questions until after Mr. Pottinger had answered hers. "Is there someone who can verify your presence at the cinema on that Wednesday night?"

"There is, but . . ." Mr. Pottinger ran a finger along his collar. "Let's just say that it would be better for her, and for me, if that was kept a secret." Mr. Pottinger did have a bit of a swagger about him, and it wouldn't be the first time infidelity had entered the equation.

"Are you a married man, Mr. Pottinger?"

Mr. Pottinger nodded. "She . . ."

Ginger held up a palm. "No need, Mr. Pottinger. Would your companion corroborate your whereabouts?"

"If necessary," Mr. Pottinger said gruffly, "but in this country, one is innocent until proved otherwise."

"I apologize for putting you on the spot," Ginger said. "I'm only trying to do my due diligence."

With a sigh, Mr. Pottinger relented. "If it comes down to it, I will involve the lady, but only if absolutely necessary. Now, are you going to tell me what happened to Farnsworth?"

"Someone blinded him. Completely this time."

Richard Pottinger's reaction took Ginger by surprise. He laughed.

"Mr. Pottinger, I don't see the humour in this."

"My apologies, Mrs. Reed." He wiped his mouth as if to erase his smirk. "Are you sure he's really blind?"

Ginger unleashed her astonishment. "He most certainly is blind. I saw his eyes. Both irises have been completely destroyed."

"Oh." The smirk faded from Mr. Pottinger's face. "I do apologize. I didn't know he had actually sustained an injury."

"Are you suggesting you had suspected him of deceit?"

"This will sound shocking, Mrs. Reed, but I saw him walking down an alleyway in Bristol like one who could see naturally, quickly, unconcerned about footpath obstacles, sidestepping a drunk. He had his cane, but he was carrying it over one shoulder, stepping onto a high curb with barely a glance. He actually stood to read a sign that hung over the entrance to a pub before he entered it. He reached for the door handle without any effort. There was no doubt that he could see it clearly, and at that moment, my suspicions were confirmed. Roland Farnsworth was a fraud."

Mr. Pottinger paused to light a cigarette. After releasing a smoke-filled puff, he continued, "When I returned to London, I contacted a chap from Farnsworth's unit who knew him rather well, having served in the trenches with him. He knew quite a lot about Farnsworth's medical conditions. It turns out he did receive treatment for a blow to the head and lost his sight for a time, but the attending doctor noted on the records that he expected Farnsworth to fully recover his sight as there was no damage to the optic nerves."

Ginger waved fingers through the smoke -filled air. "Why didn't you confront Mr. Farnsworth in Bristol?"

"I almost did but thought better of it. As soon as he had seen me, he would have put on the act, and it would be his word against mine."

"If it's true that Mr. Farnsworth was faking his blindness, I can assure you that he is no longer. The question remains as to why someone would commit such a vicious act against him, and more to the point, who?"

"My guess would be someone who took issue

with Farnsworth's duplicity. There's no question his career has benefited from his ruse."

"Did you obtain any evidence to support your accusations?" Ginger asked.

Mr. Pottinger blew a long plume of smoke out of the side of his mouth and looked around for an ashtray which he found on the nearby window sill. "I'd been watching him, and he knew it. Unfortunately, that caused him to perfect his act. I thought if I could get my hands on his spectacles, I could take them to an optician and have the prescription checked. I suspect they are fake." He scoffed. "One can hardly steal the glasses off a blind man's face. I thought I had a chance when he once left them on his desk during a short visit to the loo. He returned just as I was holding them up to look at them. For a brief moment his eyes latched on mine, dark with fury, before he resumed the blind act. Finding his desk with his cane, he lowered himself into his chair and grabbed at his desk top with his fingers, as if to search for the spectacles he knew were in my hand. He had the audacity to say, and quite loudly, 'Can you help me find my spectacles, old chap?'

"My colleagues were watching by this time, and I had no choice but to hand them back. I whispered, 'You're very good at this act.' His eyelashes fluttered, but he kept his gaze floating forward, and never said a word in reply."

"Have you discussed your theories with anyone else?" Ginger asked.

Mr. Pottinger shook his head. "No. To make such a claim, I needed concrete proof. Farnsworth isn't liked here at the paper, but he is respected for his work. Can you imagine the splash a story exposing him would make? Ha! It would be in every newspaper in the country."

"Your resentment is rather evident," Ginger said. "Perhaps this is why Mr. Farnsworth named you as a possible suspect."

Mr. Pottinger huffed, releasing smoke through his nose. He stabbed the ashtray with the butt, extinguishing it. "That's not surprising. He would like nothing better than to frame me or implicate me somehow."

"If what you say is true, why do you think he did it?" Ginger lifted a questioning brow. "Convincingly faking blindness, day in and day out, would be frightfully difficult."

"He owes his success as a journalist to his *supposed* blindness. How do you think he manages to get all these interviews? Celebrities, athletes, even heads of state all have some degree of sympathy or another, and once you get an interview with one person of note, it snowballs into more. His trademark is his blindness. Every celebrity now likes the idea of granting an interview to the famous blind reporter from *The News Standard Weekly.*"

"It's my understanding that you were recently granted a coveted interview," Ginger said. "Is that due to the fact that Mr. Farnsworth has been unable or unwilling to work?"

Richard Pottinger leaned in. "I may get some better assignments with him gone, but I still have to chase them all down one by one. I work on my own merit, Mrs. Reed. Besides . . ." he relaxed into his chair and tented his nicotine-stained fingertips over his soft midsection, "how do you know he didn't do this to himself?"

3

*G*inger mentally replayed the interview with Richard Pottinger as she eased the Crossley onto Fleet Street. The notion that Mr. Farnsworth might have self-inflicted those terrible wounds was absurd. However, the psychology of the human mind was often confounding. A man of sufficient instability once cornered, could be possessed to do unthinkable things, even radical self-harm.

The question was, was her client mentally unstable? Certainly, many a soldier returned from the war a changed man, and Mr. Farnsworth had sustained a head injury that made it credible it could have affected him in that way.

Perhaps he had indeed begun his career with

legitimate blindness, and if this *novelty* did open doors, Ginger could see the temptation to continue with the ruse if his eyesight began to improve.

Magna had dredged up an address for Mrs. Sophie Radford, Mr. Farnsworth's one time liaison. Ginger parked the Crossley across the road from the red-brick terraced housing in a quiet middle-class area of Clerkenwell.

She reached the front door and used the iron knocker, but no one answered. A second attempt failed, and Ginger was about to abandon her quest when the entrance to an adjoining house opened and an older woman stepped out. Then, much to Ginger's surprise, a Boston terrier trotted out onto the porch. The breed was an American creation and Ginger wasn't used to seeing dogs in London that resembled Boss so closely.

"Good boy, Wallace." The woman fussed with her keys. "Just let me lock up."

"That is an exceptionally handsome dog," Ginger said with a smile.

"Oh, thank you." The woman squinted at Ginger through her spectacles.

"Yes, I have a Boston terrier as well," Ginger said. "The same colouring and size. I call him Boss."

The woman chuckled. "That's a good name. I bet he's a good dog."

"He is that. I'm very fond of him."

"I'm very fond of my Wallace too. Unfortunately, not everyone around here likes dogs." She nodded to her neighbour's door where Ginger stood.

"My name is Mrs. Reed, but some know me as Lady Gold from Lady Gold Investigations."

"My lady." The woman offered a slight curtsy. "I'm Mrs. Cotterill."

"I'm looking for Mrs. Radford," Ginger said. "I'm told she lives at this residence."

"She does indeed. She volunteers at the Colville Society's Used Clothing shop, just down the road from here. I'm going there now. You're welcome to come along."

The cool weather kept them from chatting too much, and they kept the pace as brisk as Mrs. Cotterill was able.

"Have you lived in your house a long time?" Ginger asked.

"Yes, milady. A good twenty years." She cast Ginger a sideways glance. "But you're back in London after a long time away, aren't you? I read the society pages."

"It's true," Ginger said. "I spent my formative

years in America, but I'm back in England for good now."

They reached the shop, and once inside Ginger gave the woman a cheery, "Very nice to chat with you, Mrs. Cotterill." She then asked an attractive woman in her mid-forties, standing behind the counter, for Mrs. Radford. The clerk stared back with curiosity. "I'm Mrs. Radford. And you're Lady Gold!"

Ginger was used to people recognizing her from time to time, but she was certain she'd never met Sophie Radford before. "Do we know each other?"

"No," Mrs. Radford said, a rosy bloom appearing on her cheeks. "I've seen you at Feathers & Flair, though you probably wouldn't have noticed me. I bought a nice pair of leather gloves recently. I'm surprised and honoured to see you here in our humble little shop. How can I be of assistance?"

Ginger cast a glance at Mrs. Cotterill browsing one of the racks. A small bulge under her cape was the only indication that she was hiding a small dog underneath it, and Ginger felt a renewed affinity for the woman. She inclined her head toward Mrs. Radford. "Might we speak in private?"

Sophie Radford's open expression disappeared. Her arched brows furrowed as her hands nervously smoothed out the fabric of her day frock. "I'm needed at the cash desk."

Ginger made a show of glancing about the near-empty shop. Only Mrs. Cotterill and one other lady were present, and both appeared occupied. "It won't take long," she said.

Mrs. Radford guided Ginger to a sparsely furnished but comfortable office at the back of the shop. Neither made an attempt to sit, and Ginger got right to the point. "I understand you and a gentleman known as Mr. Roland Farnsworth were once involved."

Mrs. Radford scowled. "I can hardly imagine what this has to do with you, Mrs. Reed."

Ginger considered Mrs. Radford's change in address, first referring to her as Lady Gold and now as Mrs. Reed. The woman really did know who she was.

"You might know that I work as an investigator on occasion. Mr. Farnsworth is a client."

"I see. Yes, well it seems that he's told you that already, and it's true. But that was some time ago. Why is this coming up now?"

"Mr. Farnsworth has been the victim of a serious crime."

"What happened?" Mrs. Radford asked. "Was

he robbed or something?" She flicked her hand. "Never mind, I don't want to know."

"He was physically attacked," Ginger said. "I'd like to get a picture of the man beyond what he himself has told me. Since you were once close to him, I thought you might be able to give some insight."

Mrs. Radford's shoulders relaxed. "I can try. He's blind, but I imagine you already know that."

"Who ended your relationship?" Ginger asked.

After a slight hesitation, Mrs. Radford said, "I did."

"Mr. Farnsworth told me he broke it off."

Scoffing, Mrs. Radford said, "I'm hardly surprised. The man suffers from a chronic case of overblown self-importance, and it shows in how he treats others, which is poorly. I admired him as someone who had overcome a handicap, but I refused to be mistreated."

"Mistreated how?" Ginger asked.

"He has a low opinion of the weaker sex. Perhaps his blindness makes him feel vulnerable around other men, but around women, he can still feel powerful." Mrs. Radford cocked her head as she considered Ginger. "It's probably why he hired a lady investigator."

LEE STRAUSS & NORM STRAUSS

Ginger stiffened. She'd like to have believed she was sought out because of her reputation as an investigator, and that her sex had nothing to do with it, but perhaps that was naive.

"He's a man who makes his living with words, Mrs. Reed," Mrs. Radford continued. "He used them as a sword against me. Cutting me down and bruising my confidence. It wasn't that hard to walk away."

"There are some that believe Mr. Farnsworth faked his blindness, or at least misrepresented the severity of his condition," Ginger said.

"Who said *that*?" Mrs. Radford demanded.

"Richard Pottinger, a colleague." Ginger tapped her thigh with her long nails. "Do you know him?"

Mrs. Radford shook her head. "No."

"Did you ever question his disability?"

"I hardly thought to question it," Mrs. Radford answered. "Roland claimed he could see shapes and things, but only as shadows. I had no reason to question it. I mean, Roland couldn't cross the street on his own, or read anything unless it was in Braille. When his articles came out, I always read them back to him."

Mrs. Radford's gaze darted to the office door, and Ginger sensed her eagerness to return to her post at

34

the cash desk. "Mrs. Radford, do you have any idea who might have attacked Mr. Farnsworth?"

Mrs. Radford shrugged a thin shoulder. "Roland has interviewed a few powerful people, and I suppose if one of them didn't like the way his report was written, they might've retaliated." She took a step towards the door. "At any rate, Lady Gold . . ." she said, returning to Ginger's titled name, "Roland Farnsworth is not a subject I enjoy talking about. I've wasted enough time on that man. Now if you'll excuse me . . ."

"Of course," Ginger said, "but one last thing, please. Protocol dictates that I ask you where you were when the attack happened, which was on February the fifteenth."

Looking a bit perturbed by the question, Sophie Radford nonetheless reached into her pocket and removed what looked like a small diary. She flipped through the pages, stopping at what must've been February.

"I was in Cornwall visiting my cousin Fran. I try to do that once a year. It's really quite lovely there."

Ginger nodded her appreciation. She'd task Magna with trying to prove or disprove Sophie Radford's alibi.

4

_W_hen Ginger arrived at the office of Lady Gold investigations the next morning, she found Magna at her desk, which sat adjacent to Ginger's own.

"Good morning, Ginger," she said as she scooped up a manila folder. "And to you, Boss."

Ginger hung up her coat while Boss happily trotted over to his wicker basket. "What have you got here?" she said, taking her seat at the desk.

"Just a few things I found in my scratching about yesterday." Magna handed over the folder. "It's nothing earth-shattering. But before we dive into all that, I would like to hear what _you've_ uncovered." Magna grinned slyly. "Let me guess. Are the _communists_ involved? I don't trust those Bolsheviks one bit.

One of those socialist thugs could have done it. Or was it a vindictive playwright or union boss? Did you have your Derringer with you yesterday?" she added, referring to Ginger's Model 95 pistol that she often carried in her bag. "I don't have a licence yet, as you know."

The last phrase was a reference to an ongoing discussion Ginger and Magna had been having about enlisting Basil's help to gain Magna a licence to carry a gun. So far, the powers that be had deemed that Magna had 'no sufficient reason' to carry a sidearm which irked Ginger's assistant greatly. She had applied thrice and had been turned down each time even though, like Ginger, she was a crack shot and had carried a weapon with her for most of the war. Magna's hope was that Basil could 'pull some strings', but the chief inspector had so far proved to be reluctant to use his position to do so.

"That's probably why you send me on these research errands, isn't it?" Magna continued snidely. "I'm without a weapon."

"I send you on those errands because you're good at them," Ginger said. "As for getting you your sidearm licence, if you would just submit to taking that small firearms course first, you might have a better chance at getting a pistol. Basil doesn't know you like I do. He doesn't know your background and I'm not allowed to tell him."

Magna huffed.

"Believe it or not, I didn't have to pull out my pistol once yesterday," Ginger said with a smile. "And, as far as I can tell, there are no communists involved."

"What a shame."

"But I did find out a few things that you might find interesting." Ginger related Richard Pottinger's theory that Mr. Farnsworth had been faking his previous condition and that his present wounds could be self-inflicted.

"An astonishing hypothesis." Magna leaned back in her chair. "He'd have to be very desperate to do such a drastic thing to himself." She shook her head. "I don't believe it. Even in his damaged state, the man oozes pride and arrogance. He'd never willingly put himself in a position of discomfort or disfigurement."

Magna had in the past proved herself to be a good judge of character, and today as well, Ginger had to agree.

Magna pushed stray black locks off her pale face. "The mystery is why would such a man come to us to investigate? Especially if that were the case."

"Indeed," Ginger said. "And if Mr. Pottinger had exposed Mr. Farnsworth, it would have been the story of the year in London, and a very scandalous end to Mr. Farnsworth's illustrious career and good reputation."

"Our best theory is that the perpetrator would have known he was faking it all those years, and for reasons we have yet to identify, sought to make the condition authentic so to speak," Magna said.

Ginger shrugged. "But why would anyone attack someone's eyes if the victim were, to all intents and purposes, already blind?"

"Well, the only person we know who suspects Mr. Farnsworth was faking his condition is Richard Pottinger."

"Still, the motive isn't sitting right with me," Ginger said. "Mr. Pottinger wanted to expose Mr. Farnsworth. It would have been a big story and a triumph for Mr. Pottinger. Now that chance is gone."

Magna nodded. "It would be very difficult to prove past deceit now that Mr. Farnsworth is truly blind."

"Indeed."

"Did you learn anything from your interview with Sophie Radford?"

"She claimed she ended the relationship with

Mr. Farnsworth," Ginger said, "not the other way around. She's in agreement with Mr. Pottinger, when it comes to Roland Farnsworth's character. It seems our client is not particularly well liked by those who know him best. Mrs. Radford doesn't agree with Mr. Pottinger's suspicions about Mr. Farnsworth's previous condition though. She believes his blindness prior to this attack was authentic."

"An interesting contradiction," Magna observed.

Ginger returned her attention to the folder on her desk. "Now, what have you got here?"

"I spent most of the day at the London Library looking for archived newspaper stories and interviews involving Roland Farnsworth," Magna said. "He's interviewed everyone from our illustrious Prime Minister, Mr. Asquith, to Charles Lindbergh. Every interview was what I would call 'softball', to borrow an American term. No hard questions were asked, no challenges of any kind, ensuring each interviewee would be pleased with the results."

"Mr. Pottinger alluded to this tactic." Ginger leafed through the various articles.

"As for Sophie Radford," Magna started, "she's the widow of the late Dr. Herman Radford, a prominent physician who had his surgery in a house in Clerkenwell."

"That's where she lives now, in Clerkenwell," Ginger said.

"The couple devoted a lot of time to charity, and the good doctor used his clinic to treat those unable to afford normal health care. I found several references to them in the news including this one." She handed Ginger a photograph from a newspaper clipping. It was a short article in *The Daily Telegraph* from July of 1921 which reported on the couple's active work in charity.

"Mrs. Radford continues to support charitable endeavours," Ginger said. "I found her working at a charity shop."

"Herman Radford died in 1923 of brain cancer." Magna's steely eyes shone with a curious gleam. "And here's an interesting fact. He lost his sight. Apparently, he was almost completely blind during the last two years of his life."

The familiar feeling of a growing hunch started to form in Ginger's mind. "Too great a coincidence to be ignored, I'd say."

Magna nodded. "As would I. I also enquired of my contact at the Met, who was kind enough to help me."

Without looking up from reading the newspaper

clippings, Ginger enquired, "Were the fluttering of eyelashes involved in any of that?"

"I'm sure I don't know what you mean," Magna returned, coyly.

"Hmm." Ginger raised her eyebrows in response but kept on reading.

"Anyway, Sophie Radford was Sophie Wright before she married Dr. Radford," Magna continued, "and here's something: a Sophie Wright was arrested in 1918."

Ginger stopped reading and looked up. "On what charge?"

"Assault. She spent eight months in Holloway Prison for attacking her former flatmate with a fire poker. The attack was apparently unprovoked. My contact didn't know much more than that, and the records don't state a motive. The flatmate spent time in hospital but survived without permanent injuries. Perhaps Mrs. Radford's marriage to Dr. Radford reformed her. She seems to have devoted her life to helping the less fortunate."

"Perhaps," Ginger muttered, but her attention latched on to an article about a charity event from the year before. She pointed at it as she glanced back at Magna. "What's this?"

Magna craned her long neck to see the article in

question. "Oh, that's a public ceremony to commemorate the opening of that used clothing shop in Clerkenwell."

The grainy photograph accompanying the write-up had been taken from the side. One man, dressed in a suit and trilby hat, had a large pair of scissors in his hand and was about to cut a ribbon that was strung across the entrance to the building.

Ginger withdrew a magnifying glass from her desk drawer and held it over the photograph. Without looking up she asked, "Was there any sign of forced entry at Mr. Farnsworth's flat?"

"None. Whoever did it must have slipped in while he was sleeping."

"He said he locked it every night," Ginger muttered, squinting through the glass.

"He must have forgotten that night."

"Or someone had an extra key made when they had it in their possession." Ginger straightened and stared at Magna. "I've been thinking about the way the attack happened. Subduing a man using chloroform would involve a struggle. The assailant must be strong enough to hold the victim still for a few moments until they succumb to the fumes, even if they are attacked while sleeping."

"So, our perpetrator is a male."

Ginger tapped her finger on the photograph. "Unless the crime was committed by more than one person."

Magna walked around her desk to get a closer look at the image in the newspaper. Ginger handed her the magnifier.

Ginger knew what her assistant would see. In the small crowd watching the ceremony, not far from the front, was Sophie Radford. She leaned towards the man beside her, whispering directly into his ear. Ginger spoke in Magna's direction. "It's Richard Pottinger."

Magna's dark brows arched high. "*Oh là là.*"

"Mrs. Radford told me that she didn't know Mr. Pottinger," Ginger said.

Magna snorted. "Clearly, Mrs. Radford was lying."

5

*L*ater that afternoon, Ginger knocked on the front door of Sophie Radford's house, and this time it opened after only a few moments. Mrs. Radford stared back with apprehension.

"Good afternoon, Mrs. Radford," Ginger said. "Please forgive our unannounced visit." With a nod to Magna she added, "This is my associate, Miss Jones." A wave to Boss, who sat obediently at Ginger's feet, was followed by, "This is Boss."

Mrs. Radford's look turned sour. "I'm afraid I don't get along that well with dogs. That one looks like the nuisance which lives next door. It's always growling at me."

Ginger scooped Boss into her arms. "My dog is very well behaved. You won't even notice him. Might we have a few words?"

Mrs. Radford shivered at the open door and wrapped her arms around herself for warmth. "I don't know what we would talk about. I told you I'm not particularly fond of talking about Mr. Farnsworth, and I have nothing more to say."

Magna levelled her steely-blue eyes on the woman. "There are new developments in the case. We believe you'll be interested in what we have to tell you, Mrs. Radford."

"It will only take a moment," Ginger pressed. "It's very important and we would really appreciate your help."

"Very well." Sophie Radford motioned for them to step inside. Soon they were sitting in a nicely decorated parlour, with Ginger and Magna sitting on a sofa and Boss lying down obediently at Ginger's feet.

Mrs. Radford disappeared into the small kitchen located just off the living room to put a kettle on. When she returned, she sat on the edge of a matching armchair, looking agitated.

"You lived in this house with your late husband, didn't you?" Ginger asked.

"I did."

Ginger inclined her head. "I understand he was a physician."

Mrs. Radford grimaced. "You've done your homework, I see."

"We have," Ginger concurred. "To confirm, his clinic was situated at this residence."

"Yes, not that it's any of your business." Mrs. Radford stuck her nose in the air. "I thought you had information for me. If I'd known I'd be interrogated, I wouldn't have invited you in."

Ignoring the woman's outburst, Ginger asked, "Did you assist him at all?"

"Well, I'm certainly not a trained nurse, but I did help a bit, yes. I was happy to assist my husband. He was a good man and did his best to help heal people."

"How, exactly, did you assist your husband?" Magna asked.

Mrs. Radford's eyes narrowed as her lips tightened, and Ginger feared they were about to be thrown out. "We're getting to the point, if you'll have some patience," Ginger said softly.

"I organized his appointments, greeted the patients, that sort of thing. Nothing medical, of course."

"We understand you spent some time in Holloway prison," Ginger said.

Mrs. Radford's cheeks paled then blossomed red in indignation. "Forgive me, Mrs. Reed, but you are barking up the wrong tree. I'm beginning to believe you suspect me of something underhand. I've already told you I was away on the night Mr. Farnsworth was attacked." Her voice tightened with growing irritation. "As for spending time in Holloway prison, it was a one-time incident. I was young and foolish. I'm not now. End of story. Now . . ."

Ginger interrupted. "In our last conversation, I told you that someone believed Mr. Farnsworth was faking his blindness."

"And I told you what I thought of that theory."

"You also told me you didn't know Richard Pottinger." Ginger nodded to Magna who then produced the newspaper photograph of the grand opening of the clothes shop.

"You might need this." Ginger drew her magnifying glass out of her handbag and held it out to Mrs. Radford. The woman stared at Ginger without taking the instrument. She barely even glanced at the paper. Clearly, she was familiar with the image.

"If we searched your residence, specifically the room that your husband used for his practice, would we find leftover supplies stored in it?"

Sophie Radford stared at Ginger with wild eyes.

"Would we find an atomizer?" Magna added. "Perhaps a jar of chloroform?"

"How about a duplicated key for Mr. Farnsworth's flat?" Ginger asked.

Mrs. Radford found her tongue. "I'm sure I don't know what you're talking about!"

"We tracked down your cousin Fran, in Cornwall," Magna said. Ginger didn't blink as Magna spoke the lie. Sometimes a small fib was all it took to dislodge the truth.

"I need to take care of the tea." Mrs. Radford sprang up from her seat and headed towards the kitchen door.

Ginger raised a brow at Magna.

A moment later they heard the sound of the front door opening. At the same moment, Boss jumped up and, in a blur of black and white, streaked through the parlour.

"Mon dieu!" Magna shouted.

Ginger shot off the sofa and ran towards the entrance.

"Wallace!" The sound of the neighbour's voice came through an open window. "What on earth!"

Before Ginger reached the door, she heard the sound of barking dogs. Magna joined her on the doorstep. For a moment, they stood open-mouthed at the improbable scene before them.

Two nearly identical Boston terriers had Sophie Radford pressed up against a brick wall, barking and growling as if they had cornered a fox.

GINGER JOINED Basil in the sitting room for an evening digestif, their shared preference being brandy.

Curled up together on the settee, with a fire burning brightly in the stone fireplace and Boss snuggled in at her side, Ginger let out a contented sigh. Basil swirled his brandy in the glass twice before taking a long sip, then he closed his eyes as he leaned his handsome head back.

"Busy day?" Ginger enquired.

Basil lifted his head and steadied his warm hazel eyes on her. "Yes, it was. But you've been busy too, haven't you? I'm getting used to your name being bandied about in connection with some crime or another committed somewhere in our fair city."

A small smile played across Ginger's lips. "Consider it my way of reminding you of me, your dear and loving wife."

Basil squeezed her shoulders. "Other wives send a favourite sandwich in a bag with perhaps a little note attached."

"How droll." Ginger sipped her brandy then gave Basil the highlights of her case of the blind reporter.

"Was Farnsworth surprised at the outcome?" Basil asked.

"He certainly was." Ginger twirled a strand of her red bob around one finger. "He couldn't believe his former lover would have anything but good will towards him. But the man does suffer from a certain lack of awareness."

"To know him is to love him, eh?"

"I believe that's the way he sees it."

"The police are rounding up the accomplice this evening," Basil said.

Ginger nodded. "Richard Pottinger."

"How did the two schemers meet anyway?" Basil asked. "Do you know?"

"Mrs. Radford and Mr. Pottinger met at another charity event shortly after Mr. Farnsworth had 'dropped her like a hot potato'." Sophie Farnsworth had become a right chatterbox when she was cornered, hoping to lay all the blame at Mr. Pottinger's feet. "They found a common interest in their hatred for Mr. Farnsworth, both believing he was faking his blindness."

"Have you asked Farnsworth about his supposed blindness, from before his attack?"

"Yes, but he denies it. However, Sophie Radford says she caught him reading the daily news when he thought she wasn't looking. I suppose we might never know for sure, but in this instance, she has no real reason to lie."

"And I understand the motive was just sheer animosity."

"A woman scorned," Ginger said. "And also, having been married at one time to someone who had dedicated his life to helping the less fortunate, including the blind, and dedicating her own life to charitable efforts, she just couldn't bear the thought of a successful man like Roland Farnsworth pulling the wool over everyone's eyes."

"How noble of her," Basil said dryly. "Clever turn of phrase, by the way, my dear."

"Thank you, love," Ginger said with a grin. "Mr. Pottinger was sufficiently taken with Sophie Radford and jealous enough of Mr. Farnsworth's success to agree to sneak into his flat with the help of a key, secretly duplicated by Mrs. Radford. He applied the chloroform, and once Mr. Farnsworth was subdued, Mrs. Radford sprayed acid into the man's eyes."

Basil lifted his glass of golden liquid and regarded it as if it were a crystal ball. "What a romantic way to spend an evening."

Ginger reached over to pat Boss on the back. "We can't forget Boss's contribution to apprehending the villain. Along with his new friend Wallace."

"Jolly good job, Boss," Basil said, but despite the high commendation from one of Scotland Yard's chief inspectors, the cadence of Boss' snoring did not alter in the least. Basil grinned at Ginger. "Did Magna shoot anyone?"

Ginger raised a brow. "You know she doesn't have a pistol."

"Did she choke anyone?"

"Of course not."

"Judo chop to the shoulder or any places of exposed soft tissue?"

"Not that I know of."

"Explosives?"

Ginger rolled her eyes.

Basil chuckled in response. "A boring week for her, then."

"*Basil!*"

"All's well that ends well." Basil raised his glass. "Cheers to another *peacefully* solved mystery at Lady Gold Investigations."

———

THE CASE OF THE
MURDEROUS WIFE

1

January 1928

Mrs. Georgia Reed, Ginger to her friends, was hiding from the wrath of winter with her assistant, Magna Jones, in the office of Lady Gold Investigations.

Magna, with her raven-dark hair cut short and pressed like a helmet against a shapely head, read aloud from the daily newspaper. "The flood water has been drained from the Tube lines, and debris cleared from the Embankment, but there's a row between the local and central government over who should take responsibility."

"I've had quite enough of weather trauma," Ginger said. "The poor souls who didn't make it."

Magna flipped the pages. "If you'd rather hear about the fluff pieces, there's an article in here on how to get Clara Bow's hair style and make-up, or you could see a hypnotist fleece the gullible, if you like that sort of thing."

"Don't you?" Ginger asked.

Magna let out a snort. "It is utter nonsense. Only the weak-minded would let themselves be taken in by such foolishness."

"Oh, I don't know," Ginger said. "Some of the things I've heard . . ."

Magna pierced Ginger with her signature steely gaze and changed the subject. "Are you still considering going to St. Moritz for the Winter Olympics?"

In spite of appearances, it was a harmless question. Magna could stare a grown man twice her size into submission with that look, and Ginger avoided locking eyes with her as much as possible.

"Heavens, no." Ginger blew on her cup of Earl Grey. "Basil and I are in agreement that we have seen enough snow for a while."

Heavy snow starting late on Christmas Day had turned into a nationwide blizzard. This, combined with an unusually warm and wet beginning to the new year, caused the river Thames to breach its banks. A good part of central London had flooded overnight. Even though Ginger's offices in Mayfair were well away from the riverside districts that had been devastated by the flooding, Basil had hired an emergency work crew to place a wall of sandbags around the entrance to Ginger's office and her Regent Street dress shop, Feathers & Flair, as a precaution, since water had entered the underground railway systems.

"We seemed to have escaped ruination," Ginger continued. She pointed to the plush red rug on the wooden floor and then waved her hand at the beige and gold-accented walls.

Sitting in one of the wine-coloured leather chairs facing Ginger's walnut desk, Magna sipped coffee, then said, "It's probably a good thing you're not going to Switzerland. Not if you wanted to cheer your home team. I don't place much hope in Britain winning any Olympic gold medals at St. Moritz."

"You surmise that Belgium will do better?" Ginger returned with a raised brow. Belgium was Magna Jones' proclaimed place of birth, but Ginger couldn't be sure of anything Magna said if it was connected to the war. She and Magna seemed to be complete opposites in every way, but they did share a history working together as secret agents against the Germans. It was an unwritten rule not to speak of it.

Magna blinked slowly, then, without answering the question directly, said, "I've read that the Canadians have ice hockey pretty much dominated. The Americans are looking very strong for the bobsleigh, *and* the Swedes are putting forth a stellar figure skating team." She nodded towards the high windows and the grey sky that could be seen above. "The British just don't seem to have this ice and snow stuff quite mastered yet, do they?" Magna's Belgian-French accent was soft, but unmistakable. So was the wry smile on her lips.

Ginger had to agree. "I fear not, but Basil thinks we have a chance at tobogganing."

Magna's eyebrows came together in puzzlement. "Before this Christmas, had you ever even seen a British person on a toboggan?"

"Not often," Ginger admitted.

At that moment, Boss, Ginger's beloved Boston terrier, lying in his wicker basket in the corner, let out a big snore.

Magna lifted her cup towards Boss and chuckled. "I agree, Boss. We could use a bit of excitement, couldn't we?"

As if Bossy, even in his sleep, had sensed the coming adventure, the bell above the door chimed. Ginger and Magna turned towards the sound and watched as a young lady, carrying a wet, black umbrella, stepped into the office. The hem of her day frock peeked out from her raincoat. Trim brown hair framed a plain but pleasant face.

Ginger stood at her desk. "Can I help you?"

"Good day. I am hoping you can, as a matter of fact."

"Please take a seat." Ginger gestured to the matching leather chair beside where Magna had remained seated.

Boss raised his handsome black-and-white head and regarded the young lady with sleepy curiosity. Ginger always considered Boss' reactions when a new person came through the door of her office. Over the years, her pet had proved to be an excellent judge of character. In this case, he sniffed with indifference, then closed his round brown eyes as he rested his head on his front paws.

"You look like you could use a cup of coffee," Magna said as she put her cup down on the desk. "Or would you prefer tea?" She stood up to move to the kitchenette.

"Why, thank you," the lady said as she unravelled a bright red woollen scarf from around her neck. "Tea would be nice. It's rather soggy outside today." Then to Ginger she said, "You must be Lady

Gold. You look just like the photographs I've seen of you in the rags, though I didn't realize you had such red hair."

"Black-and-white images do keep one guessing," Ginger said. "Most people call me Mrs. Reed."

"Mrs. Reed it'll be then. You're married to a police officer, aren't you?"

"Chief inspector, "Ginger corrected. "Clearly you've done your homework on me."

"Yes, well, it seemed prudent. My problem is rather, er, delicate."

Ginger was well acquainted with the delicateness of most of her clients' problems. This attribute was usually why people sought out her services, rather than the police.

"Perhaps we can start with your name?" Ginger said gently.

"Certainly. I'm Mrs. Henderson. Eleanor Henderson."

Magna returned from the kitchenette with a tray containing a fresh pot of tea and a single cup and saucer.

"We only have condensed milk," Magna said, setting the tray within reach of their potential client.

"That's fine," Mrs. Henderson said. "I prefer it black."

Ginger continued with the introduction. "Mrs. Henderson, this is my assistant, Miss Jones. Now why don't you tell us what brought you here today."

"Well, I was intrigued to learn that London had a working *female* private investigator."

Ginger tilted her head. "Is that important to you?"

"No, not especially. It's just that I believe a woman would be more intuitive to my problem."

"Oh?" Ginger returned. "How so?"

"My husband Neil and I have been married for three years. And, until recently, it had been going splendidly." She sighed heavily, her shoulders slumping with the weight of her burden. "I would've said we were very happy."

"You suspect he is having an affair, and you want Mrs. Reed to investigate," Magna offered.

Ginger grimaced inwardly. Magna was very good at what she did, but sometimes she lacked tact.

"No," Mrs. Henderson said with a sharp shake of her pretty head. "Neil is not having an affair. In many ways, that would be simpler. I'm afraid it's even more serious than that. You see, my husband has lost all trust in me."

"I'm not a marriage advisor, Mrs. Henderson,"

Ginger said, keeping her voice soft. "If you're the one having the affair, might I suggest . . ."

"No . . . no. I'm sorry I am not making myself clear. He doesn't trust me for what could be a good reason."

Ginger and Magna both stared at the woman.

"And what might that reason be?" Ginger prompted.

Mrs. Henderson squirmed under Magna's narrowed gaze and settled her worried eyes on Ginger. "Apparently, Mrs. Reed, I tried to kill him."

2

Ginger dipped her chin and raised a brow "You tried to kill him?"

"Allegedly." Eleanor Henderson blew on her tea.

Ginger and Magna shared a look. It wouldn't be the first time one spouse had attempted to murder another, but they'd never had one come to them and admit to the crime.

"Allegedly?" Magna said. "Surely you would know whether you attempted to kill your own husband or not."

"That's the thing." Mrs. Henderson set her teacup down. "I don't remember doing it."

"When did the alleged incident occur?" Ginger asked.

Mrs. Henderson replied, "Four days ago."

"Amnesia, then?" Magna prompted.

Ginger also wondered if amnesia could be blamed. She'd recently taken a case where the client had suffered from a form of amnesia caused by mental trauma from the war. But this woman seemed too young to have been involved much in the war in any way.

"It seems to be the logical conclusion," Mrs. Henderson said. "The doctors are befuddled, and to be frank, so am I. I've been of a perfectly sound mind until this happened."

"So, you don't think you actually tried to kill your husband?" Magna clarified.

Mrs. Henderson pinched her red lips. "No. I can't imagine such a thing."

Ginger leaned in. "So . . . you don't *want* to kill your husband."

"Heavens no," Mrs. Henderson said. "I love him."

"Did the police get involved?" Magna asked.

"Oh yes, I was arrested."

"But . . . you're not in prison," Ginger observed.

"No, they let me go. There was no motive found, and my husband dropped all charges."

"Please start from the beginning," Ginger said.

"What actually happened to your husband that led him to believe you wanted him dead?"

"Was it your cooking?" Magna said.

Ginger shot her assistant a scolding look.

"I had a friend in Antwerp who should have been arrested for her *Mosselen met friet,*" Magna returned defensively, looking back at Ginger. "And it's not a big jump to suspect poison."

"It was his bicycle," Mrs. Henderson said. "Apparently, I may have sabotaged his brakes. Neil works for a bank in central London, and he rides his bike to work every day. We live near Shetlands Lane."

"That's a long hill," Ginger said.

"Yes," Mrs. Henderson said with a slight tip of her nose. "We live near the start of the decline. Neil lost control a quarter of the way down and hit a tree. He broke his arm, fractured some ribs and badly scraped his left shin. An ambulance had to be called. Thank goodness he didn't get hit by a car or something."

Magna's steely eyes flashed. "Are you saying your husband lost control of his bicycle and blamed *you* for it?"

Eleanor Henderson glanced away as she murmured, "Yes."

"Who discovered the defective brakes?" Ginger asked.

"A bobby on his beat happened to see the whole thing. He's the one who called the ambulance and the one who noted that the brake pads were stripped away." Mrs. Henderson looked pleadingly at Ginger. "Neil is meticulous with his care of his bike. There's no way he would have let those brakes come loose on their own, and even if he had, the pads wouldn't have been missing."

"Why did the police decide you were at fault?" Ginger asked. It was natural, when a violent crime appeared to be domestic in nature, to look at the spouse, but Ginger wanted to hear Mrs. Henderson's explanation.

"Our neighbour came to visit Neil in hospital. He told my husband that he had seen me going into our shed in the early hours of the morning of the incident. This was before Neil usually awoke."

"Did you?" Ginger asked.

"No. I sleep until it's time for me to make breakfast for my husband. He has to be at the bank by nine, so he leaves around eight to get there in plenty of time."

"It's your word against his," Magna said.

"Yes, well . . ." Mrs. Henderson sighed before

continuing. "My footprints were found all around in the mud and dirt by the shed. Neil asked the police to check on that immediately. It had rained a lot that week and any footprints would have been easily seen. I saw them myself after Neil told me. It was true, and I hadn't gone to the shed in weeks. I don't have any reason to, as there are only his bicycle and a few garden tools used in the summer months in there." With a perturbed look, she continued, "The prints matched my winter wellies perfectly."

"Sleep walking, perhaps?" Ginger offered.

"If so," Mrs. Henderson said, "it was the first and last time."

Ginger let out a long breath. This was a most unusual situation, and she was uncertain if she should get involved. This woman appeared to be afflicted with a medical or psychological ailment. Perhaps she had hidden aggression as a result of a troubled childhood. Ginger wasn't a psychiatrist and wasn't eager to delve into an area that she had little experience in. She could refer Eleanor Henderson to a trained expert in the matters of a troubled mind.

"Where do things stand now exactly?" Magna asked.

"As I mentioned before, my husband dropped the charges and the police have subsequently dropped the investigation. Neil says he still loves me and doesn't want to see me in jail. But our relationship has changed considerably. He doesn't trust me anymore and hardly speaks to me."

"Mrs. Henderson," Ginger began, "I don't know if I'm the right person to help you with this. I . . ."

"Someone tried to kill my husband, Mrs. Reed. That's attempted murder. Now I don't know why anyone would do such a thing, but I know deep down inside it was not me. I'm being framed."

Ginger watched as the young woman's eyes welled up. Her hands trembled as she dabbed her tears with a handkerchief.

"Please, I don't know where else to turn." Like her hands, Mrs. Henderson's voice was also shaking. "You're a woman, and married, I'm assuming to a good man. Think about what it would be like if this happened to you."

Ginger exhaled as she stared at Magna who gave a subtle shake of her head, indicating her opinion: *Don't take the case.*

Staring back at Mrs. Henderson's pleading eyes, Ginger found she was intrigued, and a perplexing case like this would stimulate her mind.

"All right, Mrs. Henderson, I will look into it."

3

*T*he next morning Ginger drove her white 1924 Crossley west towards Hampstead Heath. Boss, who sat next to her on the passenger side, sat on his haunches staring out the side window, his pink tongue extended.

As was her custom, she drove at a brisk speed. The Crossley was a joy to drive, and Ginger was always keen to push it to its limits of manoeuvrability.

"Almost there, Bossy." Ginger honked her horn impatiently at a lorry that lumbered in front of them, forcing Ginger to step forcefully on the brake pedal. Poor Boss slid with a yelp onto the floor in front of the seat.

"Boss, are you all right?" Her pet jumped back

onto the seat, his round brown eyes bright as if he'd already forgotten the excitement. When he panted, his little face always looked as if he were smiling, and Ginger smiled back. "No harm done."

Once she reached the base of Shetlands Lane, she slowed considerably, ignoring the irony as two cars behind her now sounded their horns with impatience.

"Don't worry about them, Boss," Ginger said glibly. "I need to see if I can spot the tree where Mr. Henderson crashed his bicycle."

About two-thirds of the way up she found an oak tree such as Eleanor Henderson had described, near a sharp curve. With a wave in her side-view mirror to the cars behind her, she pulled into a nearby alley.

After instructing Boss to stay, she climbed out of the motor car and walked towards the tree, which was a good twenty feet tall with a sturdy trunk rising from a grassy square in the pavement. Most of the upper part of Shetlands Lane was bordered on one side by a high brick wall that looked like it had been built after the war, protecting the traffic from the steep drop on the other side. This particular section of the hill, however, was not walled in. For safety, there were small metal posts erected in front of the break in the wall to prevent a motor vehicle from going through. A runaway bicycle, however, would not get any benefit from the narrow posts.

A thin, newly formed scar could be seen extending from the front of the tree, at the right height to have been formed by the handlebars of a man's bike.

After closely examining the grass around the tree and the trunk itself for a few moments, Ginger made her way back to the car.

"Well, Boss. That tree stopped *someone's* bicycle." Boss looked at her with his head cocked to one side, as if asking if she'd learned anything more. Ginger was quick to let him know. "I found this button not far from the tree." Opening her palm to further examine a brown button, she added, "Probably from a waistcoat or jacket. Could be anyone's, I suppose."

It was a short drive up the rest of the incline to the Hendersons' home, a terraced house of red-brick construction. Ginger parked in front of the house and once again commanded Boss to stay. This time though, she covered him with his favourite blanket for warmth. These days he was content to stay in the car as long as he was kept warm. She walked back the short distance to the top of the lane and stared at the view of the hill, then after fishing her notepad and pencil from her handbag, she quickly sketched what she saw.

Instead of proceeding to the Henderson residence, Ginger went next door to the neighbour's house, and knocked on the front door.

A man in his sixties answered. He had a long white beard, unkempt white hair, and was dressed in a brown cardigan, Oxford bag trousers and black leather slippers. The wild-looking hair wasn't the most striking thing about him though; he was very possibly the shortest man Ginger had ever met other than a circus performer. He brought to mind a kind of gnome with his long beard. Thick glasses made his blue-grey eyes look as large as billiard balls.

In his left hand he held a newspaper as if he had just been disturbed in his morning reading.

"Yes?" he asked, his voice gruff.

"Good morning," Ginger started. "I'm Mrs. Ginger Reed of Lady Gold Investigations. Are you Mr. Fairfax?"

The man's magnified eyes widened further. With conspiratorial intensity, he stepped outside and stared next door at the Henderson residence. Then he stared back at Ginger.

"You're here about the attempted murder, aren't you?"

"*Alleged* attempted murder," Ginger corrected. "Yes, I am. Could I have a word?"

Mr. Fairfax waved her into the house. "Please come in."

His house was in a state of disarray of the untidy variety rather than the unclean, though the air smelled strongly of cigarette smoke. Mr. Fairfax led Ginger up a short flight of stairs to a sitting room on the next floor. It was cluttered with magazines, throw blankets, and a large ashtray on a side table that was in need of emptying.

"Crumpets!" The man pointed his finger in the air in front of him as though he'd been struck with a brilliant thought. "My charlady baked some this morning, and she just put the kettle on for tea before she left!" He pivoted sharply without waiting for a response from Ginger and disappeared, leaving Ginger standing in the middle of the room.

An odd little man, Ginger thought as she looked for a place to sit. After clearing a space on a wing-back chair, she sat and took in the room.

Single, was the first thought that came to her. *Perhaps never married.*

Without any warning a large grey tabby cat suddenly jumped onto her lap

"Oh mercy!" The cat settled down on her lap,

making himself at home. Within a moment he was purring loudly and blinking sleepy, green eyes at her.

She stroked the feline's soft furry head. "Seems as if you've got me trapped."

Mr. Fairfax returned with a tray that was brimming with tea, crumpets and jam.

"You didn't have to go to all that trouble, Mr. Fairfax," Ginger said.

"No trouble at all," Mr. Fairfax said as he set the tray down on the coffee table. "I'm always happy to have an excuse for a second breakfast." His eyes narrowed in on the cat on Ginger's lap. "Stone the crows!" He waved his hands emphatically. "Tommy, get off her now."

Startled, the cat jumped off Ginger and slinked under the chair.

"I'm not bothered by the cat," Ginger said, a little belatedly for the circumstance. "He might be smelling my dog on me though." She clasped her hands and rested them on her lap. "I will abstain from the tea, if you don't mind. Can I ask you, Mr. Fairfax, do you live alone?"

"Except for Tommy, yes. I never did marry, you know. I was in love several times, but . . ." He let out a long sigh. "It never worked out. Women find me too eccentric." He spread butter on half a crumpet and stuffed almost the whole piece into his mouth, crumbs dropping onto his white beard. His huge eyes stared curiously at Ginger as he chewed.

"I take it you're retired."

Mr. Fairfax nodded as he folded short arms over his round chest. Ginger wanted to reach over and brush the crumbs from his beard but focused on his large eyes instead. Mr. Fairfax continued, "I was an accountant and was lucky enough to make some good investments after the war, so I was able to retire earlier than some."

"Good for you," Ginger said.

"Good for you too," Mr. Fairfax said. When Ginger gave him a surprised look, he nodded. "A lady private investigator. Brilliant."

Ginger removed a notepad from her handbag. "How long have you known Mr. and Mrs. Henderson?"

"Well." Mr. Fairfax attempted to cross his leg at the knee, giving up after one try and crossing his ankles. "I don't really *know* either of them. Mr. Henderson lived here for a year before he married. We've only spoken on rare occasions. So, to answer your question, I have been acquainted with him for about four years and with her around three."

"Can you tell me what you saw on the morning of Mr. Henderson's bicycle incident?"

"I saw what I saw, plain as day right out of that window." Pushing himself out of the chair, he trotted to the window. Ginger followed him.

His position afforded a clear view of the Hendersons' small back garden.

"The shed door was open, and Mrs. Henderson was there, as clear as day, dressed in her housecoat and wellies." He clicked his tongue. "She's not the type to get up early so must believe no one else does either. She didn't even bother to close the door to hide what she was doing."

"What time was it?"

"Six thirty. Well over an hour before Mr. Henderson usually retrieves his bicycle."

"You're saying that you saw Mrs. Henderson attending to her husband's bicycle at six thirty in the morning?"

"Yes, madam. It wasn't even light at that time. She was using a torch to see. Made it easy for me to see too. She knelt beside the bike with a tool. *That*, I couldn't make out, but my curiosity was jolly well piqued. A few moments later, she closed the shed door and returned to the house."

"You said you didn't interact with the Hendersons very often, inferring you were friendly but not friends. Can you tell me why you visited Mr. Henderson in hospital?"

"I felt it was my duty to tell him what I had seen."

"Have you seen Mr. and Mrs. Henderson argue, or act acrimoniously towards each other in the past?"

"No, never. Mind you, I'm not the kind to make my neighbours' business my own."

Ginger forced a placid look. "Of course not, Mr. Fairfax." She summoned a smile. "Thank you so much for your time." Ginger returned to her chair to collect her handbag.

"Leaving already?" Mr. Fairfax said. "You haven't even had a crumpet."

Ginger sensed the little man was hungry for companionship. "I'm frightfully sorry," she said kindly. "I have quite a lot of work to do today. But if you don't mind, I might call on you again if I have more questions."

"Yes, yes, of course." Mr. Fairfax sounded disappointed as he turned and stared back out the window.

As Ginger was about to leave, she noted a worn and frayed waistcoat hanging on a coat rack by the door. Four buttons hung loosely from their threads, and one was missing.

The buttons looked exactly like the one she had picked up by the tree where Mr. Henderson had crashed his bike.

She checked to see if Mr. Fairfax was watching, but he had yet to follow her. With a quick tug she tore loose one of the buttons, palming it just as Mr. Fairfax joined her at the door.

"Forgive my slowness," Mr. Fairfax said. "My old mind likes to wander, and I lose track of time."

"That's quite all right," Ginger said. "I have one more question. Do you often walk down the hill here on Shetlands Lane?"

Mr. Fairfax shook his white head. "Oh no. These legs can't take that long incline. I take a motor bus if I need to go into London."

"But have you seen the spot where Mr. Henderson crashed?"

"Actually . . . no, I haven't," Mr. Fairfax said, his large eyes narrowing as he stroked his beard, crumbs from his crumpet finally dropping to the floor. "But," he continued, "I know that it is a dangerous route for cyclists, especially for those without brakes."

4

Ginger parked the Crossley in a discreet place where she might not be noticed by Mr. Fairfax should he emerge from his front door, as it turned out that he did not fifteen minutes later. He stiffly walked down the street in the opposite direction of the hill and disappeared around the corner.

"I won't be long, Bossy." Ginger patted her dog's sweet head, then gave him a treat from the supply she kept in her handbag.

Ginger had always made a point of enquiring about her clients' daily schedules in case there was a need of surveillance, which was how she knew that Mrs. Henderson would be busy at her weekly hair salon appointment. It had happened to Ginger before that she had actually been hired by the perpetrator in an effort to misguide and misdirect, so it was pertinent that she got to them as best she could. And by best, she meant when they weren't around.

Ginger knocked on the front door of the Henderson house, the last in the row, just to make sure, but as expected, there was no answer. She decided to start her search with the shed which she had to access from the back alley. Using her lock-picking kit—a speciality item from her time as a British intelligence agent in France during the Great War—she opened the padlock.

After she had slipped inside the shed, she rolled the various lock picks back into the oiled leather cover, then traded them for the torch she also carried with her. Her eyes adjusted to the dim light which came through small windows. Various garden tools hung from the wall, along with watering cans and a pair of dusty gloves. A black, men's bicycle leaned against a work bench, the front wheel bent and the handlebars twisted awkwardly to the right. Eleanor Henderson had told Ginger that since the incident a few days earlier, Mr. Henderson had understandably not gone back to his bicycle. It might take some time before he would gain the courage to go back down that hill, even once the apparatus had been repaired and his bones had thoroughly healed.

On the down tube of the frame were painted the words 'Coventry Royal'. The machine appeared to be of a high quality and well maintained, the leather on the seat oiled and smooth, and even the chain wheel was spotlessly clean. Like most bikes of this type, the brakes were operated by pulling on a spring-loaded bar that ran parallel to the main handlebars. It was a simple but effective design. When one pulled on the spring-loaded bar, it in turn tugged on cables which then caused small twin rubber brake pads to squeeze against either side of the metal wheel. Those brake pads were supposed to be affixed to metal callipers by means of a small nut.

The saboteur must have loosened the nuts to the point of almost falling off. The misdeed would have gone unnoticed at first, and the brakes could have worked for one, perhaps two applications, but after that, the brake pads would have surely fallen away. The rider might have heard a sharp squealing sound as the metal callipers uselessly squeezed the rim of the wheel.

Completing her examination, Ginger turned off her torch, pausing to peek outside through a small window. She stopped short at the sight of Eleanor

Henderson's profile in the kitchen window that faced the back. She'd come home sooner than expected, forcing a delay in Ginger searching the premises.

Once the coast was clear, Ginger secured the padlock then returned to the back alley and strolled swiftly towards her motor car. She was reasonably certain she had not been seen.

"THAT WAS QUITE POSSIBLY the most boring day I've ever lived through," Magna said as she climbed into Ginger's Crossley that same afternoon and pulled Boss onto her lap. "There's nothing quite like watching a banker do . . . well, nothing, for an entire day."

Ginger let the hyperbole go unchallenged. She was sure Magna had been on plenty of assignments that were less eventful than this one. She slipped the motor car into gear. "He must have done *something!*"

"No, nothing. Unless you call sitting at a desk, reading papers, signing, yawning, sipping tea, occasionally stretching . . . unless you call that something. *Mon dieu,* that man has a boring job!"

Mr. Henderson, having left the bank, loitered at

the nearest motor bus stop, waiting for the next machine to arrive.

"The only suspicious thing he did today was to not get up to use the lavatory for a solid four hours."

"And what did you do for all that time?"

"Pretended to read the newspaper in the lobby. Except that I did leave for a few moments to use the lavatory."

"We knew it was a long shot," Ginger said. "But you do remember it was *your* idea to watch the fellow?"

Magna huffed. "The last time I ran surveillance on someone, it was a German *Oberstleutnant* in 1918. He was meeting with a suspected French collaborator who was giving him a secret list of names. I was found out and had to escape by scaling a wall, swimming across a river, hiding in the forest, and shooting a German soldier in the forehead with a slingshot." Magna's lips twitched into a subtle smile as she patted Boss on the head, seemingly enjoying the memory.

Ginger shot Magna a sidelong glance. "I'm afraid that working at Lady Gold Investigations is unlikely to hold the level of derring-do that we both experienced back then. It's a bit more sedate than being a spy during wartime." Ginger suddenly swerved the

LEE STRAUSS & NORM STRAUSS

Crossley to the left to avoid a slow-moving horse and carriage.

"That is certainly true," Magna returned. "But the occasional ride with you in the motor car does tend to elevate the pulse quite nicely. Perhaps I need to do that more often if I want to relive the thrills of yesterday."

Ginger raised a brow. It was the first time anyone had ever expressed a preference for her driving style.

"At noon, the target . . ."

"The word *target* is rather aggressive," Ginger protested.

"At noon, the *mark* took lunch at a sandwich shop around the corner. I followed him in and bought a ham sandwich."

"No sense starving on the job." Ginger shifted into a lower gear to climb the incline of Shetlands Lane. "Did you eavesdrop?"

Magna snorted. "Of course I did. I sat at the table across from two businessmen who tried to chat me up. Very droll of course, but I did manage to get snippets of Mr. Henderson's conversation with one of his work colleagues. Unsurprisingly, that conversation was not exactly riveting, but I did hear him say that he was not in favour of his wife's naturopath. Apparently, she sees one once a week."

"It's curious that she didn't bother to mention that when I asked for her schedule," Ginger said.

"Perhaps because naturopathy is regarded as quackery by many, including her husband."

"Were you able to ascertain why Mrs. Henderson felt compelled to engage a naturopath?"

Magna dropped her chin in a subtle nod. "Mr. Henderson was kind enough to explain it to his friend. His wife suffers from joint pain in the knees. Even though Mrs. Henderson claims the man helps her manage her pain, Mr. Henderson thinks the man is a charlatan and far too expensive."

"Did he mention a name?" Ginger asked.

"Unfortunately, not."

"Hmm . . ." Ginger worked her lips. "There must be at least a dozen naturopaths in London right now."

"He didn't exactly sound like a fellow who was in love with his wife, either," Magna said. "He said she was getting on his nerves."

Ginger considered Magna's comment. "Do you think he staged the whole thing? Sabotaged his own brakes?"

"It would make a good excuse for a divorce." Animated, Magna lowered her voice. "*I suspect my wife tried to kill me, but I can't prove it absolutely. I don't trust her anymore."*

"He dropped the charges against his wife, when he could've left her in jail," Ginger said. "Besides, if he meant to frame her, he'd have to give her a plausible motive."

"Perhaps there's life insurance?" Magna offered. "Or he caught her having an affair. What if she has a violent past or is insane?"

"I suppose we'll have to dig a little deeper," Ginger said.

The tram they were following came to a stop and Ginger slowed behind it. They spotted Mr. Henderson's familiar form and watched him get on a motor bus.

"That motor bus goes up Shetlands Lane," Ginger said. "It looks like he is heading home."

"Banker's hours." Magna glanced at her wristwatch. "Don't get me wrong, I'm glad his workday is over earlier than most working men's."

Ginger glanced at her timepiece as well. "It's only half past three."

"Tell me you found something exciting at the Hendersons," Magna said.

When the traffic slowed, Ginger reached into her bag, pulled out two brown buttons and held them out in an open palm. "I found one on Shetlands Lane at a very strategic spot. The other one was about to fall off the very worn waistcoat of the Hendersons' neighbour, Mr. Fairfax, the rather peculiar man who claims he saw Mrs. Henderson sabotage her husband's bicycle. "

Magna examined the two buttons. "Cheaply made from Bakelite. Identical, but these are produced in quantity I think, so there's no way to know for sure. I suppose they could've come from the same garment."

"Notice how the button I found on the ground is clean, as if it had only recently been dropped there. No scuffs or any signs of being trodden upon."

Magna nodded then settled her steely gaze on Ginger. "What kind of sedative did you use?"

Horrified, Ginger blurted, "I didn't use a *sedative!* I just plucked it from the waistcoat when he wasn't looking. Good heavens, Magna, he wasn't wearing it at the time."

"It's just that waistcoats aren't usually left by the front door but are hung in one's bedchamber when disrobing."

Magna had a point, but she hadn't met the strange little man, and Ginger could imagine him impulsively removing the sleeveless garment should he feel heated, no matter the time and place.

"The point is," Ginger said as the traffic picked up again, "he claimed he never walked down the hill and hadn't seen the tree, but if the button is his, then clearly he is lying. However, if we see him as a suspect—and whoever planned this sabotage has an intimate knowledge of Shetlands Lane—then we have to uncover his motive."

Ginger slowed as they reached the tree where the accident had occurred. "That's where it happened."

"Shetlands Lane is very steep," Magna noted, her eyes taking in the hill ahead. "But an out-of-control cyclist would be all right until that curve."

Ginger agreed. "Directly on the outer part of the curve, the part where the momentum of the bike would take you, is a steep drop. There is a break in the fencing with no curb, and parking is prohibited on that side of the lane, so there are no vehicles to act as a barrier either."

Magna's eyes flashed with understanding. "The saboteur calculated the precise spot, *that gap,* where the cyclist would lose control of the bicycle and veer off course and plunge to his death."

"Or hit the tree," Ginger said. "It is just beyond

that critical point. In other words, either Mr. Henderson's cycling skills saved his life, or the brake pads held on for one more application. He was able to somehow—and this must have been very hard to do—steer his bicycle into the tree instead of going over the edge. When you look at the spot where this happened, it seems almost impossible that Mr. Henderson managed to hit the tree."

Magna mused, "So the killer was gambling."

"Yes, it wasn't a sure thing. I think the killer walked down there, made some careful calculations and decided to go ahead with it."

Ginger kept her distance as the motor bus stopped and Mr. Henderson stepped off and crossed the street to his residence.

"Did you search the shed?" Magna asked.

"Yes," Ginger said, "but I didn't find anything conclusive, only that the brake pads were missing and that the tools to accomplish loosening them were readily available there. It's not a difficult task if one knows what to do."

Magna opened her door. Surprised, Ginger asked, "What are you doing?"

"I've got errands to run. I'll just catch the next motor bus. See you in the morning?"

"All right," Ginger said. She couldn't very well

tie her assistant down. Nor was Magna working by the hour. She had a right to her own schedule and to her privacy.

Magna disappeared on the next bus. Ginger was about to follow it when she saw movement at the Henderson residence. Mrs. Henderson appeared, then walked to the end of her street where a black taxicab had stopped and was waiting.

Ginger waited for Mrs. Henderson to climb in and for the taxicab to drive away.

"Hold on, Bossy." Ginger pulled sharply on the wheel, turning her Crossley around to follow.

5

The taxicab stopped in front of a row of residences in Camden Town. Mrs. Henderson exited, paid her driver, then climbed the steps to one of the doors, which appeared to be unlocked as it opened with her knocking. She slipped inside with the confidence of someone who has entered the premises many times before.

Ginger, parking several motor car lengths back, was too far away to see the sign hanging on the door.

"Fancy a walk, Boss?"

Ginger fastened the leash to Boss' collar, opened her umbrella, then took him for a stroll. The streets and pavements were glossy from the ongoing precipitation, but mercifully the rain had slowed to a drizzle.

Before long, they were passing the door Mrs. Henderson had entered, and the sign was clear: Simon Teale ~ practitioner of Natural Medicine ~ Operating Hours 9-5 weekdays.

Returning to the Crossley, Ginger wiped Boss' paws with the towel she kept under the seat for that purpose, then retrieved her camera.

The camera was a new Vest Pocket Autographic Kodak camera which used 127 film and was slim enough to fit inside her jacket pocket. It would have come in handy during the war years, but they were new on the market back then and hard to come by.

Ginger had been waiting for an hour when the figure of Mrs. Eleanor Henderson emerged from Simon Teale's office. She climbed into a taxicab that had arrived just minutes before. Ginger was about to head inside to meet this Simon Teale fellow herself, but as providence would have it, a bookish-looking man of around the age of forty emerged, wearing a winter jacket. Ginger had her camera ready and snapped a few pictures of the man as he locked the front door behind him, then came down the steps.

Setting the camera aside, Ginger exited the Crossley and called out, "Dr. Teale?" even though she was fairly certain he wasn't a real doctor. She had the right man as the fellow came to a sudden stop and turned towards her voice.

"Yes, that's me," he returned cautiously.

On closer inspection, Ginger noted that the naturopath was rather frail-looking, with wispy brown hair and a pale complexion.

"I'm Mrs. Reed from the office of Lady Gold Investigations. Do you have a moment? I would like to ask you a few questions."

"Well, I . . ." Simon Teale glanced back at his office. "I'm afraid I'm closed for the day." He took a step back. "Ring my office in the morning, and we can make an appointment."

Ginger ignored the man's attempt to elude her. "I'm investigating an incident to do with Mrs. Eleanor Henderson. I believe she is a patient of yours."

"Mrs. Henderson . . . yes, she is." His small blue eyes darted up and down the street, as if to ensure that Mrs. Henderson had really gone. "I really am in a bit of a hurry."

Simon Teale began to walk away, and Ginger fell into step after him. "It's about an accident that happened to her husband, Neil Henderson."

"I'm afraid I've never met the man and have had

no dealings with him and with regards to Mrs. Henderson. I'm afraid I cannot discuss my patients with anyone. Now, please, if you'll pardon me, I have nothing else to say."

THAT EVENING GINGER sat with Basil in the drawing room, enjoying a sip of brandy. It was a favourite part of her day, and she loved it when their schedules allowed for time alone to relax in front of the fire. She snuggled into Basil's side, sharing the settee with him and Boss, who didn't like to be left out of the trio. Her dog eyed her with round brown eyes filled with affection as he rested his chin on her thigh.

"Is that another grey hair, ol' boy?" Ginger said as she scrubbed him behind the ears. "I suppose none of us is getting any younger, but I do hate to see it on you."

Basil pulled her in close and Ginger sighed with contentment, safe and warm in her abode, knowing her children were well a floor above.

Her mind, naturally, couldn't stay off the case indefinitely, and she looked up at Basil. "Did you get a chance to question the constable who was first on the scene?"

She didn't need to specify which scene. Basil immediately knew.

"I did," he said. "He happened to be there just at the right moment to witness Mr. Henderson crashing into the tree at top speed. He didn't see the approach, just the moment of impact. He rushed to help, and when he saw Mr. Henderson had been badly injured, he directed a passer-by to summon an ambulance."

"And did he examine the bicycle?"

Basil nodded. "The brake pads were missing from their callipers. He suspected foul play immediately, either that or gross negligence on the part of the rider. Afterwards, it went exactly as you described. Mr. Henderson's wife was arrested on the strength of a witness' testimony, but later on, the husband dropped the charges."

Ginger relayed the story of her short stakeout of Simon Teale's office. "I snapped a couple of photographs."

Basil pointed his chin towards the manila envelope on the coffee table. "Is that them?"

Ginger moved to retrieve the envelope. "I developed them in the attic before dinner." She'd had the darkroom installed shortly after setting up Lady Gold Investigations. Taking photographs for clients was a large part of her job. She laid out four pictures on the coffee table between them. "I don't suppose you've come across this man before?"

Basil leaned forward and examined the images. Ginger watched as a wry smile came across his face. Then he stared at her, his hazel eyes gleaming with admiration. "My dear, you never cease to amaze me."

Ginger smiled back. "Thank you, love, but what have I done this time?"

"We've had this man under investigation for months now. He uses two names, one of which is Teale. He often uses 'doctor' as his title, but he has absolutely no credentials. We haven't arrested him for that because he never uses it formally."

"Does he have actual training in naturopathy?"

"Some. But he never completed anything that is accredited."

"I'm familiar with that branch of medicine," Ginger said, "and have done some of my own research. Sometimes the practitioners call them- selves 'health culturists', and it's a burgeoning field in America and growing here in Britain. Some sanato- riums have reached national prominence, like the one in Brighton which claims great results curing chronic diseases."

"Unfortunately, because the practice of naturopathy is a fairly recent phenomenon, it's not well regulated," Basil said, leaning back into the settee. "There's a significant amount of quackery as a result. The Yard is suspicious of a few of them, including Mr. Teale."

"Is that why he's been under investigation?" Ginger asked as she played with the rope of pearls around her neck.

"I'm afraid it's for more than that." Basil let out a short breath. "There have been two cases of fraud, one case of attempted robbery and three cases of assault in recent months, all sharing the curious trait of the perpetrator not having a discernible motive. The assault cases have all been perpetrated by wives against their husbands."

Ginger sat up. "That *is* curious."

"All of the wives involved were young and attractive," Basil added.

"Like Eleanor Henderson."

"Yes. Arrests have been made, but the cases are proving hard to prosecute when the suspects have no motive and *no memory* of committing the act."

"Again, like Eleanor Henderson."

"And you'll appreciate this," Basil said, as he set

his glass on the side table. "All the ladies involved in these motiveless crimes had been patients of Mr. Teale."

Ginger's fingers went to her throat. "Oh mercy."

"We have been having a hard time pinning anything on him because we lack any direct connection. It's all just circumstantial so far."

Ginger twisted to face her husband. "You said he has two names?"

"Yes, the other one is Armando Xavier, also known as *The Great Armando*."

"Strange names."

"For a strange man," Basil said. "He's a mesmerist."

Ginger frowned. "A stage hypnotist?"

"Once a month at various variety theatres in London," Basil said, nodding. "He wears a disguise. Police have followed him from his office to where he performs and have even sent plain-clothes detectives in to observe. But again, we haven't been able to prove any wrongdoing. But from what we can ascertain, he was a mesmerist long before he became a naturopath."

The implications were so bizarre that Ginger had to let it circle around in her mind several times before she spoke it out loud. "He hypnotizes his victims. That's how he does it. It's why they have no memory of committing the crimes." She locked her gaze with Basil's. "Ten to one, he hypnotized Mrs. Henderson too."

6

The next evening, Ginger and Magna attended the early evening showing of *London Eclectic–The city's most entertaining variety show*. The variety show played in The South End Variety House, which hadn't been renovated to accommodate films instead of live productions. The tall theatre, which was as high as the four-storey building next to it, looked worn and neglected. The once ivory-coloured paint was dingy and peeled off the Roman columns on its façade. A large, brightly lit sign announcing the show extended from the front upper-level bank of windows, and inside the lobby, thick carpeting under a high vaulted ceiling gave the feeling of grand imagination. The main auditorium held about three hundred people in two horseshoe-shaped tiers with thinning velvet seats. Ginger and Magna were seated in the first tier to the right of the curtained stage.

"Keep your eyes and ears open," Ginger said, leaning towards Magna. "I'm not sure what we'll find here tonight, but between the two of us we might spot something of use."

Magna gave a subtle nod. "I'll be like a hawk searching for a field mouse."

A smile tugged at the corner of Ginger's mouth.

"I've been to several of these shows," Magna continued. "Sometimes they have some good acts, and sometimes not so good. I have a bad feeling about the quality of tonight's line-up."

As it turned out, Magna's intuition was correct. A simple mime act was followed by a comedy skit done by two ageing actors in faded costumes. A youth dropped a juggling club into the front row of the audience, which caused snickering and a bit of swearing from the crowd, including a mournful "*mon dieu*" from Magna. An acrobatic troupe of four from the Orient, who turned out to be rather good, came next, and then a magician whose main talent was card tricks. Finally, and with great flourish, Armando the Great was introduced.

"This is the man you described to me?" Magna said, hardly concealing her surprise.

Ginger found it hard to contain hers as well. The man who boldly walked onto the stage dressed in a black cape and top hat hardly bore a resemblance to the pasty-looking fellow Ginger had approached on the street. Armando Xavier wore a thick moustache with oiled tips which extended beyond his mouth on either side, resembling, rather ironically, the handle-bars on a bicycle. Eyeliner succeeded in making his rather small eyes appear larger, and red greasepaint made his cheeks brighter. When he removed his top hat to wave it in the air, Ginger realized that he was also wearing a wig, since his wispy hair had now transformed into a thick black mane.

"Good evening, ladies and gentlemen!" he bellowed. "What I am about to do tonight should not be attempted by anyone at home, but only by highly trained specialists like myself, and under the strictest conditions. Do not be frightened by what you see, or think you see, on this stage. It is all harmless fun . . . or is it?" His laugh carried a hint of theatrical menace. "No one will be physically harmed." The side of his mouth raised in tandem with his eyebrow. "At least not that I know of." A nervous chuckle erupted from the crowd.

The hypnotist called for a group of ten volunteers, whether courageous or foolish, they were soon to learn. The men and women who ventured onstage were each handed into a wooden chair and were seated in a semicircle. Armando gave them a series of small tasks to do, such as adjusting their chair slightly to the left or interlocking their fingers over their heads for a moment. He seemed to carefully consider each one, then politely instructed six of them to go back to their seats. The disappointed, or perhaps relieved, short-lived volunteers did as they were asked.

An assistant appeared from stage left and rolled out a large wooden wheel that was affixed to a stand. It had black concentric lines painted on a white background. Armando gave it a spin, and the lines turned into spirals that seemed to move towards the middle, creating an illusion of falling into a deep hole.

Addressing the remaining participants, Armando the Great said, "Please keep your feet flat on the floor and let your eyes gaze into the wheel. By the time I count to five you will be very sleepy, and I want you to let your eyelids close."

After the count of five, the participants indeed seemed to be sleeping even whilst sitting up, their eyelids drooping and chins dropping towards their chests.

Magna whispered, "They're either very susceptible or in on the ruse."

"From this moment on, everything I say, no matter how silly it seems, will instantly become your reality." Armando the Great moved his arms with a comedic flourish. "The ability to be hypnotized shows that you are possessed of a high intelligence and creative disposition. You are all very special."

Magna rolled her eyes. "Rubbish."

Armando the Great bid the first lady, a woman in her mid-thirties, to stand, open her eyes and tell everyone in a loud voice her first name, the place she was born, and her favourite pastime. She did this without any difficulty. "My name is Elizabeth Brown, I was born in Sussex, and I love to go for long walks in the park."

Armando snapped his fingers. "Now can you say that again please?"

Suddenly, the woman appeared to be completely intoxicated, slurring her speech so badly, she could hardly be understood. "M'name is, si, is L'issie. B-b-born . . ." Armando helped her sit down, where she continued to weave back and forth as if she had just finished an entire bottle of brandy.

The crowd roared with laughter. Ginger shot Magna a look of indignation, the poor girl's humiliation now entertainment amongst strangers.

The next participant, a man in his forties, was handed a cane. After Armando snapped his fingers once, the man suddenly dropped the cane with a yelp and jumped to the side as if the cane had become a living thing. Again, there was riotous laughter from the audience.

Another participant was made to drink ordinary water but acted like it was vinegar. This same cycle was repeated several times, until Armando loudly declared, *"Sooner or later, all spells must break, so when I snap my fingers, you will awake!"*

With the snapping of his fingers, the volunteers straightened in their chairs and opened their eyes, blinking against the spotlight. Confusion settled on their faces as if they were wondering what everyone was laughing about.

"Most intriguing," Ginger said.

Thinking the show was over, Ginger was surprised when Armando made another call for volunteers. Even more shocking was the rapid movement at Ginger's side as Magna sprang to her feet.

"What are you doing?" Ginger said.

"I want to get a closer look," Magna said, as she

LEE STRAUSS & NORM STRAUSS

waved her arm enthusiastically. "This man will have no control over me."

The light of a single spotlight now shone on the spot where Magna and Ginger were sitting. Ginger tried to move out of the spotlight, but the circumference was too wide. Armando's eyes widened when he saw her, and Ginger was fairly certain she'd been recognized.

To Magna's delight, she was selected. With theatrical pomp and flair, Armando spun the wheel, commanding the volunteers to stare at the illusion it produced. He stepped in front of each person, locking his beady eyes with their unblinking ones. When he reached Magna, Armando whispered something into her ear. She stood and he handed her the cane. Everyone expected Magna to shriek with the false belief the cane was a snake, but Magna stood normally, holding the prop in her hand.

Armando covered the miss with an overly broad smile. "Sometimes we come across a person who can successfully fight against the power of suggestion. It seems I should've excused this volunteer. Is there another who'd like to take her place? Someone who's here to have a bit of fun?"

7

*A*fter the show, Ginger suggested they compare notes over a glass of wine and good *salade landaise* at a nearby French establishment.

"I made sure I followed his instructions with a look on my face that said I was completely docile and willing to please," Magna said, then lifted a glass of wine to her lips.

"Good thinking." Relieved of her winter coat, Ginger smoothed out the handkerchief layers of the skirt of her day frock. A large gold buckle rested low on the left side of her hip, an adornment to a complementary sash. "That's how he chose which participants to leave the stage. The ones that looked eager and could follow his instructions to the letter were the most open to being mentally manipulated."

"Exactly." Magna drew long fingers over her ear, tucking in her short black bob. "And then he really poured it on by telling us how special and intelligent we were. Pfft."

Ginger wondered aloud. "Regarding Armando's victims, or rather Mr. Teale's, the ones he hypnotized into committing crimes, do you think he hypnotizes them during the show?"

"That would be risky," Magna countered.

"I quite agree," Ginger said. "It's more likely that took place at his naturopath's office. Perhaps using hypnotism overtly, as a faux method of treatment, or perhaps he performed it covertly. My guess is that his victims, like Mrs. Henderson, had no idea that he'd put them under a hypnotic state."

"What an odd, evil little man." Magna sucked air through her teeth before taking another rather prolonged sip of French red wine, then put her glass roughly down on the table. "*Quel homme méchant!*"

"Careful," Ginger cautioned. "This wine is too good to spill."

"Perhaps I need a larger goblet." Magna gazed about the restaurant for a waiter.

"Our problem," Ginger began, "is that we still

lack hard evidence that Mr. Teale has enough power over someone to make them do things long after they leave his office. How strong is the power of suggestion? How long can it last?"

"And why did he do these evil things?" Magna asked. "What is his motive?"

"I suspect he uses his influence in much the same way a witch in fables would use curses. To impose their will on others for revenge or personal gain." Ginger scowled. "Perhaps, with a pretty young woman like Mrs. Henderson, he had designs to have her for his own."

Magna scoffed. "Do you think he's in love with her?"

"That, or he had an unpleasant encounter with her husband. You'll recall Mr. Henderson saying that he thought Mr. Teale was a charlatan. By the way," Ginger's eyebrows rose in curiosity, "what did he whisper to you onstage?"

Magna cocked her head. "What do you mean?"

Before Ginger could reply, the waiter arrived with their meals.

"He whispered into your ear like he did with all the participants," Ginger replied. "What did he say?"

Magna shook her head. "I don't remember him saying anything to me."

"But he did," Ginger insisted. "I saw him."

Magna looked baffled as she cut into her steak. "You must be mistaken. I never heard him say anything to me. Perhaps that's why his stupid cane didn't turn into a snake in my hands. Ha!" She lifted the first bite into her mouth and chewed, her eyes widening with approval. "*C'est bon.*"

"Excuse me, I need to use the ladies," Ginger said, looking around. She rose when she spotted the sign and walked away.

Later, Ginger couldn't decide if she'd heard a noise, or if intuition had warned her. But she had almost reached the cloakroom's door when she suddenly whirled around and ducked aside a split second before Magna Jones, steak knife held high, lunged at her.

"Magna! What on earth?"

Ginger flung up her forearm, blocking Magna's right arm, narrowly derailing what would have been a deadly stab to her chest. Magna's momentum caused her to stumble, but she quickly recovered and started for Ginger again, her eyes dark and murderous. She held the knife in her right hand like a sword and lunged forward again.

This time Ginger clutched Magna's right wrist with her left, bending it backwards and lifting it high before spinning around and grabbing it with both hands. She brought Magna's arm sharply down onto her left shoulder, forcing her to drop the knife lest Ginger break her arm at the elbow.

Magna's cry of pain was followed by a yelp coming from Ginger's own mouth. Magna's knee slammed against Ginger's back and her palm struck her on the back of her head, propelling Ginger forward. Ginger had become very proficient at self-defence techniques in her years in France, but it was obvious to her that Magna had also received a few lessons.

Magna rushed forward to pick up the knife again, but Ginger was closer and kicked it down the hall. Magna punched her right hand at Ginger's jaw. Ginger blocked it with a forearm, but barely.

Another chopping blow followed immediately. Ginger jumped backward and jerked her head out of the way.

"Magna, stop!" Ginger shouted with her heart pounding in her ears. *"What has got into you?"*

Again, Magna started forward with menace in her eyes.

In that instant, Ginger knew what to do.

"Sooner or later, all spells must break, so when I

snap my fingers, you will awake!" Ginger snapped her fingers.

Magna's eyes cleared as she stared at Ginger with bewilderment. "Ginger? Is everything all right?"

8

A few days later, Ginger was in the kitchenette of the office of Lady Gold Investigations, rummaging through the cupboard in search of Boss' dog food. "I suppose we'll never solve the mystery of Mr. Fairfax's buttons."

Magna poured coffee into two cups. "All we really know is that an odd little man is running around with not enough buttons on his waistcoat."

"I'm just glad I don't have to spend what would have been an exceedingly boring day on surveillance. Shall I deliver your coffee to your desk?"

"Yes, please," Ginger said as she walked over and poured some dog food into Boss' bowl. Following Magna into the office, she added, "I'm just glad you didn't thrust a steak knife through my heart!"

115

Magna blew over her coffee. "Yes, that would have been unfortunate. Let me say again how sorry I am about what happened. It's a very good thing you are a formidable lady, Ginger. You were when I met you in Belgium during the war, and you are still."

"As are you," Ginger said. "But let's make that the last time we engage in fisticuffs, shall we?"

"Yes, let's." Magna rubbed her right elbow. "I will also never underestimate the practice of hypnotism again. I still feel very strange about the whole experience."

The entrance door opened, and Mrs. Henderson stepped in.

"Good morning, ladies," she said. She had a smile on her face and her voice was cheery.

"Oh good, you got my message," Ginger said. "It's so nice of you to drop in." Ginger waved to the empty chair, and Mrs. Henderson took it, the whole experience giving Ginger a feeling of déjà vu.

"I'll make you some tea," Magna said, standing.

"How have you and Mr. Henderson been? Since the news has come out about Mr. Teale."

"Neil and I are doing wonderfully," Eleanor Henderson gushed. "Trust has been restored and now we are back to the business of being married and in love!"

Ginger smiled at Mrs. Henderson's joy. "I'm very glad to hear it. And is all forgiven?"

"Yes, and the funny thing is, my joint pain has gone. I believe that was also part of his hypnotic trick. You see, I went there originally for headache problems. I don't remember when it turned into treatment for joint pains."

Returning with Mrs. Henderson's tea tray, Magna said, "Hypnotherapy is still a relatively unknown science."

Mrs. Henderson added sugar to her tea and stirred. "I can never thank you enough for saving me and Neil from that monster!" She shuddered. "I can't even think of what might've happened otherwise."

"Scotland Yard has been investigating Mr. Teale for a long time," Ginger said, "but lacked any direct evidence to prove he was manipulating people to commit crimes. Mr. Teale was charged with five counts of mischief and two counts of attempted murder. Hopefully, at least one of the charges will stick. At the moment, he is sitting in a jail cell awaiting his fate."

"It was how Mrs. Reed brought me out of it." Magna said, "That's the important bit. She used the exact line that the Great Armando used to snap his subjects out of their trance. It's his trademark line and that's what the police were missing. *Sooner or later, all spells must break, so when I snap my fingers, you will awake!* When she spoke those words, I instantly stopped the assault. I have no memory of having any designs to attack Mrs. Reed. The whole event is blank to me."

"How did he get you to attack Mrs. Reed?" Mrs. Henderson asked. "And not even during the show?"

"He'd directed me to attack Ginger when he whispered into my ear on the stage. *When Mrs. Reed says 'Excuse me' and rises to her feet, you are to kill her.*"

"Neil tried to warn me," Mrs. Henderson said with regret. "I must've told Mr. Teale stories about my husband, how he rode his bike to work every day. I can't believe I was so easily manipulated."

"Take heart in knowing you are not the only one," Ginger said. "My husband predicts that as soon as this first case goes to trial, there will be a cascade of young women whom Mr. Teale liked to control coming forward to tell their story. I think it's about to get very uncomfortable indeed for The Great Armando Xavier."

"Is your husband back on his bicycle yet?" Magna asked.

"No, not yet," Mrs. Henderson said. "But he will be after we move."

Ginger raised a brow. "Are you moving house?"

"Oh yes, we are planning to buy a house on an easy bicycle route that isn't at the top of a death-defying hill."

"Ah," Ginger took a sip of her coffee, "good idea."

Mrs. Henderson finished her tea, then rose and slipped back into her winter coat. "I can't thank you enough, Mrs. Reed, Miss Jones." She pulled out a cheque book and made one out in payment.

The bell over the door rang, marking Mrs. Henderson's departure. Boss, having finished his midday snack, sat by Ginger's chair and placed a paw on her lap.

"Come on up," Ginger said, and Boss climbed onto her lap. She scratched his ears, looking over his black head at Magna. Her steely eyes were staring blankly up at the ceiling and Ginger felt a thread of concern. Her assistant wasn't succumbing to another latent command given whilst hypnotized, was she?

Ginger snapped her fingers. "Magna?"

Magna moved her gaze to Ginger. "Yes?"

"Oh, you had me worried for a moment, gazing off like that."

"Terribly sorry, *ma chérie,*" Magna returned.

"I'm just wondering how long it will be before another client walks through the door."

"I'd be happy for a bit of a break," Ginger said. "You know what they say? All work and no play makes Jack a dull boy."

Magna chuckled. "Call me *dull* if you like, Mrs. Reed."

The phone rang. Ginger was happy—Magna had something to do. Her assistant picked up the receiver of the black rotary phone. "Lady Gold Investigations," she sang out. "How may I help you?"

———

Don't miss the next Ginger Gold mystery~
MURDER AT MADAME TUSSAUDS

Murder's a pain in the neck!

Madame Tussauds, London's extravagant wax museum, reopens in 1928 to much fanfare. The horrific fire of '25, which had destroyed the wax figurines of famous and sometimes infamous characters, was news of the past. Ginger Reed and her good friend Haley Higgins are intrigued and eager to visit the museum which promises new and exciting exhibits. Of particular interest is the one on Bram Stoker's Dracula.

Hailed by some as effective literary horror and by others as unnecessarily frightening, the exhibition about the book attracts all kinds. Haley Higgins, with her forensics knowledge, is the first to notice that something is amiss, and that the beautiful figurine with two bloody holes in her neck isn't made of wax at all, but is indeed made of flesh and bone!

When a series of women are found dead in the streets of London in a similarly eerie fashion, it's up to Scotland Yard, with Chief Inspector Basil Reed at the helm, to solve the case. Can Ginger and Haley work behind the scenes to bring this repeat killer to a stop, before one of them becomes the next victim with a deadly bite?

Buy on AMAZON or read Free with Kindle Unlimited!

———

GINGER GOLD'S JOURNAL

Did you know that Ginger kept a Journal?

Sign up for Lee's readers list and gain access to **Ginger Gold's private Journal.** Find out about Ginger's Life before the SS *Rosa* and how she became the woman she has. This is a fluid document that will cover her romance with her late husband Daniel, her time serving in the British secret service during World War One, and beyond. Includes a recipe for Dark Dutch Chocolate Cake!

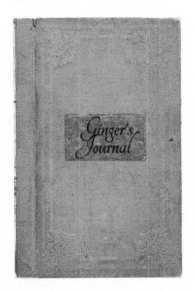

It begins: **July 31, 1912**

How fabulous that I found this Journal today, hidden in the bottom of my wardrobe. Good old Pippins, our English butler in London, gave it to me as a parting gift when Father whisked me away on our American adventure so he could marry Sally. Pips said it was for me to record my new adventures. I'm ashamed I never even penned one word before today. I think I was just too sad.

This old leather-bound journal takes me back to that emotional time. I had shed enough tears to fill the ocean and I remember telling

Father dramatically that I was certain to cause flooding to match God's. At eight years old I was well-trained in my biblical studies, though, in retro-spect, I would say that I had probably bordered on heresy with my little tantrum.

The first week of my "adventure" was spent with a tummy ache and a number of embarrassing sessions that involved a bucket and Father holding back my long hair so I wouldn't soil it with vomit.

I certainly felt that I was being punished for some reason. Hartigan House—though large and sometimes lonely—was my home and Pips was my good friend. He often helped me to pass the time with games of I Spy and Xs and Os.

"Very good, Little Miss," he'd say with a twinkle in his blue eyes when I won, which I did often. I suspect now that our good butler wasn't beyond letting me win even when unmerited.

Father had got it into his silly head that I needed a mother, but I think the truth was he wanted a wife. Sally, a woman half my father's age, turned out to be a sufficient wife in the end, but I could never claim her as a mother.

Well, Pips, I'm sure you'd be happy to know that things turned out all right here in America.

SUBSCRIBE to read more!

.

MORE FROM LEE STRAUSS

On AMAZON

GINGER GOLD MYSTERY SERIES (cozy 1920s historical)

Cozy. Charming. Filled with Bright Young Things. This Jazz Age murder mystery will entertain and delight you with its 1920s flair and pizzazz!

Murder on the SS Rosa

Murder at Hartigan House

Murder at Bray Manor

Murder at Feathers & Flair

Murder at the Mortuary

Murder at Kensington Gardens

Murder at St. George's Church

The Wedding of Ginger & Basil

Murder Aboard the Flying Scotsman

Murder at the Boat Club

Murder on Eaton Square

Murder by Plum Pudding

Murder on Fleet Street

Murder at Brighton Beach

Murder in Hyde Park

Murder at the Royal Albert Hall

Murder in Belgravia

Murder on Mallowan Court

Murder at the Savoy

Murder at the Circus

Murder in France

Murder at Yuletide

Murder at Madame Tussauds

LADY GOLD INVESTIGATES (Ginger Gold companion short stories)

Volume 1

Volume 2

Volume 3

Volume 4

Volume 5

HIGGINS & HAWKE MYSTERY SERIES (cozy 1930s historical)

The 1930s meets Rizzoli & Isles in this friendship depression era cozy mystery series.

Death at the Tavern

Death on the Tower

Death on Hanover

Death by Dancing

THE ROSA REED MYSTERIES

(1950s cozy historical)

Murder at High Tide

Murder on the Boardwalk

Murder at the Bomb Shelter

Murder on Location

Murder and Rock 'n Roll

Murder at the Races

Murder at the Dude Ranch

Murder in London

Murder at the Fiesta

Murder at the Weddings

A NURSERY RHYME MYSTERY SERIES(mystery/sci fi)

Marlow finds himself teamed up with intelligent and savvy Sage Farrell, a girl so far out of his league he feels blinded in her presence - literally - damned glasses! Together they work to find the identity of @gingerbreadman. Can they stop the killer before he strikes again?

Gingerbread Man

Life Is but a Dream

Hickory Dickory Dock

Twinkle Little Star

LIGHT & LOVE (sweet romance)

Set in the dazzling charm of Europe, follow Katja, Gabriella, Eva, Anna and Belle as they find strength, hope and love.

Love Song

Your Love is Sweet

In Light of Us

Lying in Starlight

PLAYING WITH MATCHES (WW2 history/romance)

A sobering but hopeful journey about how one young

German boy copes with the war and propaganda. Based on true events.

A Piece of Blue String (companion short story)

THE CLOCKWISE COLLECTION (YA time travel romance)

Casey Donovan has issues: hair, height and uncontrollable trips to the 19th century! And now this ~ she's accidentally taken Nate Mackenzie, the cutest boy in the school, back in time. Awkward.

Clockwise

Clockwiser

Like Clockwork

Counter Clockwise

Clockwork Crazy

Clocked (companion novella)

Standalones

Seaweed

Love, Tink

ABOUT THE AUTHORS

Lee Strauss is a USA TODAY bestselling author of The Ginger Gold Mysteries series, The Higgins & Hawke Mystery series, The Rosa Reed Mystery series (cozy historical mysteries), A Nursery Rhyme Mystery series (mystery suspense), The Perception series (young adult dystopian), The Light & Love series (sweet romance), The Clockwise Collection (YA time travel romance), and young adult historical fiction with over a million books read. She has titles published in German, Spanish and Korean, and a growing audio library.

When Lee's not writing or reading she likes to cycle, hike, and stare at the ocean. She loves to drink caffè lattes and red wines in exotic places, and eat dark chocolate anywhere.

For more info on books by Lee Strauss and her social media links, visit leestraussbooks.com. To make sure you don't miss the next new release, be sure to sign up for her readers' list!

Join my FACEBOOK READERS GROUP for fun discussions and first-to-know exclusives!

Norm Strauss is a singer-songwriter and performing artist who's seen the stage of The Voice of Germany. Short story writing is a new passion he shares with his wife Lee Strauss. Find out more at norm@norm-strauss.com

Did you know you can follow your favourite authors on Bookbub? If you subscribe to Bookbub — (and if you don't, why don't you? - They'll send you daily emails alerting you to sales and new releases on just the kind of books you like to read!) — follow me to make sure you don't miss the next Ginger Gold Mystery!

www.leestraussbooks.com
leestraussbooks@gmail.com

Made in the USA
Las Vegas, NV
01 May 2023

71344360R00083